What's Valentine's Day without someone sp
share it with? Nothing very special. I was dying for
Kyle Sullivan to be my special someone. And Joey
was going to make it happen. All he had to do was
read my valentine to Kyle on his radio show. But
then Joey started saying there wouldn't be any radio
show, all because he didn't have a special someone
of his own. I was determined to save Valentine's
Day for both of us. All I had to do was fix up Joey
with the perfect date.

You'd be amazed at the trouble you can cause by
trying to find someone their perfect match. So let
me tell you a story that won't cause trouble. The
story of my very special family.

Right now there are nine people and a dog living
in our house—and for all I know, someone new
could move in at any time. There's me, my big sister, D.J., my little sister, Michelle, and my dad,
Danny. But that's just the beginning.

When my mom died, Dad needed help. So he
asked his old college buddy, Joey Gladstone, and
my Uncle Jesse to come live with us, to help take
care of me and my sisters.

Back then, Uncle Jesse didn't know much about
taking care of three little girls. He was more into

rock 'n' roll. Joey didn't know anything about kids, either—but it sure was funny watching him learn!

Having Uncle Jesse and Joey around was like having three dads instead of one! But then something even better happened—Uncle Jesse fell in love. He married Rebecca Donaldson, Dad's co-host on his TV show *Wake Up, San Francisco*. Aunt Becky's so nice—she's more like a big sister than an aunt.

Next Uncle Jesse and Aunt Becky had twin baby boys. Their names are Nicky and Alex, and they are adorable!

I love being part of a big family. Still, things can get pretty crazy when you live in such a full house!

FULL HOUSE™: Stephanie novels

Phone Call from a Flamingo
The Boy-Oh-Boy Next Door
Twin Troubles
Hip Hop Till You Drop
Here Comes the Brand-New Me
The Secret's Out
Daddy's Not-So-Little Girl
P.S. Friends Forever
Getting Even with the Flamingoes
The Dude of My Dreams
Back-to-School Cool
Picture Me Famous
Two-for-One Christmas Fun
The Big Fix-up Mix-up
Ten Ways to Wreck a Date
Wish Upon a VCR
Doubles or Nothing
Sugar and Spice Advice
Never Trust a Flamingo
The Truth About Boys
Crazy About the Future
My Secret Secret Admirer
Blue Ribbon Christmas
The Story on Older Boys
My Three Weeks as a Spy

Club Stephanie:

#1 Fun, Sun, and Flamingoes
#2 Fireworks and Flamingoes
#3 Flamingo Revenge

Available from MINSTREL Books

FULL HOUSE™
Stephanie

The Big Fix-Up Mix-Up

Devra Newberger Speregen

A Parachute Press Book

READING

A MINSTREL® BOOK

Published by POCKET BOOKS
New York   London   Toronto   Sydney   Tokyo   Singapore

This book is a work of fiction. Names, characters, places and incidents are either products of the author's imagination or are used fictitiously. Any resemblance to actual events or locales or persons, living or dead, is entirely coincidental.

A MINSTREL PAPERBACK *Original*

A Minstrel Book published by
POCKET BOOKS, a division of Simon & Schuster Inc.
1230 Avenue of the Americas, New York, NY 10020

A PARACHUTE PRESS BOOK

Copyright © 1996 by Warner Bros. Television

FULL HOUSE, characters, names and all related indicia are trademarks of Warner Bros. Television © 1996.

ISBN: 0-671-53547-1

First Minstrel Books printing February 1996

10 9 8 7 6 5 4

A MINSTREL BOOK and colophon are registered trademarks of Simon & Schuster Inc.

Cover photo by Schultz Photography

Printed in the U.S.A.

The Big Fix-Up Mix-Up

CHAPTER
1

◆ ◀ ◗ ◆

"Slide, Cousin Stephanie, slide!"

Nicky and Alex jumped up and down with excitement.

Stephanie Tanner picked up her Chutes and Ladders piece and slid it down the chute. Her four-year-old twin cousins grinned at her. Stephanie smiled back and stared down at the board game.

Suddenly Stephanie grabbed the tissue box at her side. She scrunched up her face, then sneezed loudly into a thick wad of tissues.

"Achoo!"

Nicky and Alex giggled. "Cousin Stephanie, you used the whole box!" Nicky cried.

Stephanie gazed down at the empty tissue box. "So I did," she muttered. She pushed her long blond hair away from her face and tried her best to smile again. She felt another sneeze coming on.

This cold she had was the pits. She'd stayed home last night when all her friends went to see the new Christian Slater movie. And tonight she was stuck at home again. Saturday night—playing Chutes and Ladders with a couple of four-year-olds. And Joey.

Joey Gladstone was her father's best friend from college. He came to live with her family eight years ago—after her mom died in a car accident. Ever since Joey moved in, he'd been an important part of the Tanner family. As important as her Uncle Jesse, who had also moved in after the accident.

"Your turn, Joey," Alex cried. "Spin!"

Joey sighed and flicked the spinner. "Oooh, goody. I get to slide again. What an exciting Saturday night," he muttered. He slid his game piece down the chute.

Stephanie gazed at him in concern. Joey just wasn't himself. He kept sighing nearly every minute. It was starting to get on Stephanie's nerves. And it was sad, too. A whole hour had gone by and Joey hadn't made one single joke—or done any cartoon impressions.

Joey was always making jokes. He was a comedian and he performed on a radio show with Stephanie's Uncle Jesse. Their show was called *The Rush Hour Renegades.* Joey was always hilariously funny on the radio—and at home too. But tonight—nothing.

At that moment Stephanie's father, Danny Tanner, bounded down the stairs. He wore a navy blazer and a pair of khaki chinos. "How's this outfit?" he asked, turning around to model the clothes. "Good enough for a blind date?"

Stephanie blew her nose. "Great," she said, sniffling.

Danny leaned over to touch her forehead. "Honey, are you sure you'll be okay tonight? Maybe I should stay home and take care of you. I could make some of my famous Tanner Miracle Cure Stew. We could relax and listen to some soothing music and—"

Stephanie's stomach heaved just thinking about her dad's disgusting "miracle cure" stew. Her eyes widened and she held up her hand.

"No, Dad! Really, I'm okay. My nose is just runny, that's all. I'm feeling much better. Please, I want you to go on your date tonight."

"If you're sure—"

"I'm sure, I'm sure!" Stephanie repeated. "I'll be fine. Really. I have a big night of games planned. After Chutes and Ladders, it's Yahtzee Junior. Then Uno. And the grand finale of the evening is Colorforms."

Joey let out another sigh and everyone stared at him.

"What's up, big guy?" Danny asked in a concerned voice.

Joey shrugged. "Nothing," he replied.

"So, Dad," Stephanie said, "who is your blind date tonight?"

Danny grinned. "Well, you know my friend Elliot, right?"

Stephanie nodded.

"Well, Elliot has this friend, Wanda, and—"

"You're dating Elliot's friend Wanda," Stephanie finished.

Danny shook his head. "No. You see, Wanda has this gardener who—"

"You're dating Wanda's gardener?" Stephanie asked.

4

Danny shook his head again. "No, but Wanda's gardener's wife—"

Stephanie raised her eyebrows. "Don't tell me you're going on a blind date with the gardener's wife!"

"No!" Danny cried in exasperation. "Will you let me finish? The gardener's wife has a sister."

Stephanie waited to hear more. Then she realized her father was finished. "Oh! So you have a date with the sister!"

Danny smiled. "Elliot's friend Wanda's gardener's wife's sister!"

"What's her name?" Stephanie asked.

Danny rubbed his chin thoughtfully. "You know, I forgot to ask."

Joey stood and walked across the room. "I wish I had a date with the gardener's wife's sister," he said. "Or anyone's sister." He pushed open the swinging door to the kitchen and disappeared inside.

Stephanie snapped her fingers. *Of course,* she thought. *Now I know why Joey's so down! Valentine's Day!*

February 14 was just around the corner. And Joey didn't have a girlfriend. That was why he looked so sad. Stephanie knew just how Joey felt.

She felt the same way because she'd didn't have a boyfriend.

Joey returned from the kitchen with a glass of juice. Stephanie's older sister, D.J., came flying down the stairs. She was dressed all in black—black jeans, a black turtleneck, and black shoes. Her short blond hair was even tucked into a black baseball cap.

"Oh, no." Danny groaned. "You're not going to that weird dance club again, are you? The one where you have to wear all black to get in?"

D.J. laughed. "No, Dad, I'm not. But, for your information, that club changed its dress code. Now you have to wear all red to get in."

"So where are you going, D.J.?" Joey asked.

D.J.'s eyes lit up. "I have a date!" she said excitedly.

Joey seemed sorry he'd asked. "Great for you," he muttered, plopping down on the sofa.

"With whom?" Danny asked suspiciously.

"Relax, Dad. I met him in my chemistry class."

"How's his driving?" Danny asked.

D.J. made a face. "How should I know?" she asked. "We don't do a lot of driving in chemistry."

"Well, how do I know he drives safely?"

Danny continued. "Are you sure he isn't going to speed or something?"

"I'm sure, Dad!" D.J. and Stephanie exchanged amused looks. Stephanie and her sisters loved their father a lot, but sometimes he didn't realize what a worrywart he was. D.J. grabbed her coat and hurried out the front door.

"You should be glad for D.J.," Stephanie told her dad. "She's all excited about this new date."

Joey sighed again. "I wish I had a date with someone from my chemistry class."

"Joey, you don't have a chemistry class," Stephanie pointed out.

Danny was thoughtful for a moment. "Uh, well, listen, Joey—I suppose you could get dressed and . . ."

Joey gazed up hopefully. "And come along with you? Do you mean it?"

Danny bit his lip. "No! I mean, I was going to suggest that you—"

But Joey had already jumped up and pulled his coat from the coatrack. He ran to the front door and swung it open. "You're the best, Danny! Where are we going? Dancing? Dining?"

Danny gazed helplessly at Stephanie.

"Um, Joey," Stephanie called out, "what about

me? I need you to keep me company tonight while I baby-sit."

Joey removed his coat. "You're right, Steph. And, Danny, thanks for offering, but I suppose you should be alone on your date tonight. You don't need me hanging around, making dumb jokes." He sat back down on the floor with the twins.

Stephanie's uncle Jesse and aunt Becky came downstairs from their attic apartment. They were dressed in their best new outfits.

"Wow! You guys look great!" Stephanie cried.

Becky smiled and readjusted the strap on her high heel. "Thanks, Steph," she said as she limped across the room. "We really appreciate your staying with the twins tonight. I can't wait to try this new French restaurant."

"Hey, I know!" Joey said. "Why don't you two let *me* take *you* to dinner tonight? I owe you one, remember?"

Jesse and Becky exchanged nervous glances.

"Sure," Joey went on, "remember that time you bought me a hot dog at the hockey game? Don't say Joey Gladstone doesn't return a favor. Let me get my coat."

"Uh, Joey!" Becky called after him. "It isn't

that we wouldn't love you to come with us tonight. Really, we would."

Jesse opened his mouth to speak, but Becky stomped on his foot.

"But our table is for only two people," Becky added. "Maybe next time. I'm sorry." She grabbed Jesse's arm and pulled him toward the door.

Jesse grabbed his car keys. "We're off, then. Thanks again, Steph. We owe you."

"Big-time!" Stephanie smiled.

Jesse stopped short. "Hey! I know how to pay you back! We'll get you on the radio!"

"What are you talking about?" Stephanie asked.

"Our Teen Romance Night show. It's a new idea for Valentine's Day. Joey and I dreamed it up to boost ratings for the station," Jesse explained. "Kids can send in special Valentine's Day messages. We'll read them over the air on Valentine's night. You, Stephanie Tanner, can send one of the very first valentines."

"Great," Stephanie muttered. "But aren't you forgetting something?"

"What?" Jesse asked.

"I don't have a valentine!"

As the words left her mouth, an image flashed in front of her eyes. It was a gorgeous face. The smiling, brown-eyed, freckled face of Kyle Sullivan. Handsome, incredibly hunky Kyle Sullivan—adorable chipped front tooth and all.

Oh, no! What am I doing? Stephanie asked herself. She closed her eyes tight and tried to make the image go away. *I swore I wouldn't think about Kyle anymore. Why should I? He's not thinking of me, that's for sure. He barely knows I exist.*

Stephanie opened her eyes. It was no use. She couldn't *help* thinking about Kyle. *Wouldn't it be great*, she wondered, *if Kyle could be my Valentine?*

Then she'd have a totally perfect Valentine's Day. Kyle would show up on her doorstep with flowers and candy. He'd whisk her away for a romantic pizza dinner. And after that, a walk in the park . . . maybe an ice cream . . .

". . . and Joey can take it down to the station for you," Jesse was saying. "The deejay will read all the messages starting at six o'clock. You never know, Steph. A valentine like that could be the perfect way to let that someone special know you care."

Stephanie snapped back to reality. "Uh, thanks, Uncle Jesse, but I'm boycotting Valentine's Day this year. For lack of a valentine."

"There's still enough time to find yourself one," Jesse said with a wink. "Who knows? Maybe you'll get lucky!"

CHAPTER
2

◆ ◢ ◗ ◆

Becky grabbed Jesse's arm and pulled him toward the door. "Bye, everyone. Have a nice night! Thanks again, Steph!"

"Au revoir," Jesse added in French as the door closed.

Joey frowned. "I guess I would have been a third wheel, huh?" he asked. "They don't need me hanging around either. Nobody needs me."

Stephanie smiled at him in sympathy. *No doubt about it*, she thought. *Joey was definitely bummed about not having a girlfriend.*

Danny gave Joey a playful punch in the arm. "Don't worry. Things will change. You'll see."

He checked the time, then walked to the bottom of the stairs and called out. "Michelle! Hurry! I'm ready to go!"

Michelle, Stephanie's nine-year-old sister, ran downstairs carrying a video game cartridge.

"Let's go, sweetheart," Danny said. "Joshua is waiting."

"Joshua?" Joey frowned. "You mean even Michelle has a date tonight?"

"It's not a date," Michelle told him. "We're just friends!"

As soon as Danny and Michelle left, Joey slumped on the sofa again. "I can't believe this! A nine-year-old is going out while I sit at home."

"I know how you feel," Stephanie said. "I'll probably end up with Comet as my Valentine's Day date." She patted the family's golden retriever on the head. Comet tried to lick her hand.

"Don't count on it," Joey told her. "I have first dibs on Comet that night. You'd better get yourself another Romeo, Juliet."

Joey played one round of Uno, then turned to the twins. "Listen, guys, I'm kind of tired. I think I'll just call it a night. Okay?"

Nicky and Alex pouted.

"Hey, why the long faces?" Stephanie asked them. "You've still got me!"

"Yeah!" Alex cried. "And Stephie never wins at Uno!"

Joey smiled at Stephanie. "Thanks, Steph," he whispered. He headed upstairs to his room.

Stephanie lost four games of Uno before announcing it was time for bed. She ushered the boys upstairs and helped them into their pajamas. She stood guard as they brushed their teeth, then tucked them in. As soon as their eyes closed, she rushed back downstairs. She grabbed the phone and called her best friend, Allie Taylor.

Stephanie had met Allie nine years earlier, on their first day of kindergarten. Their teacher had sat them next to each other, and from that moment on they were fast friends. Allie had gentle green eyes and wavy brown hair. She was a lot like Stephanie, but different too. For instance, they both loved music, reading, and funny movies. But Stephanie was also a great dancer, while Allie was pretty much a klutz.

"Allie? Hi, it's me."

"Stephanie! Thank goodness! I'm going bonkers!"

Stephanie laughed. "Why? What's wrong?"

Allie lowered her voice. "Guess who's moved in with us."

"Who?" Stephanie asked.

"My aunt Wendy!" Allie replied in a hoarse whisper.

Stephanie remembered meeting Allie's aunt Wendy. She was young, pretty, and lots of fun. "What's so bad about that? Your aunt Wendy is great."

"*Used* to be great," Allie corrected Stephanie. "Now she's just a royal pain."

"Allie! What are you talking about? What happened?"

Allie groaned. "Aunt Wendy just broke up with her fiancé," she explained. "She was supposed to get married next month. But she showed up on our doorstep last night, crying her eyes out. Now the engagement is off!"

"No wedding?" Stephanie asked.

"No wedding," Allie replied.

"Wow, that's a bummer," Stephanie said. She spied a copy of *San Francisco Scene* magazine on the coffee table and started flipping through it while they talked.

"It gets worse," Allie continued. "Aunt Wendy also lost her job yesterday. So she's a total mess! She just walks around the house sniffling and crying. And when she's not crying, she's on the phone fighting with her boyfriend—I mean her ex-boyfriend. It's crazy!"

"Mmmmm," Stephanie mumbled, staring at the magazine.

"And get this," Allie went on. "I have to share my room with her! Can you believe it? My mom wants me to be extra nice and all. She even asked me to stay in on weekends, to keep Aunt Wendy company!"

"Yeah, that's too bad," Stephanie replied. But she was only half listening.

"Stephanie! Did you hear what I said?" Allie asked impatiently.

"Yeah, Allie. I heard you. You have to share a room with your aunt Wendy. Well, maybe it won't be so bad. Maybe—" Stephanie suddenly stopped short. She sat upright on the sofa and stared at the magazine. "Oh, wow! This is perfect!" she cried.

"Perfect?" Allie asked in confusion. "What's perfect?"

"Listen, Allie," Stephanie cried, "I'm sorry,

16

but I have to go. Don't be mad. I'll call you tomorrow. I promise!"

She hung up the phone, then tore a few pages out of *San Francisco Scene*. *Absolutely perfect!* she said to herself. "Joey will be dating again in no time!"

CHAPTER
3

♦ ◂ ◾ ♦

Stephanie shoved her desk chair under the bedroom doorknob. She gave it a hard push to make sure it was wedged in tightly.

"Is that really necessary, Stephanie?" Darcy asked.

Darcy Powell was Stephanie's other best friend. Darcy and her family had moved to San Francisco from Chicago in the middle of sixth grade.

Stephanie would never forget Darcy's first day at school. Darcy had plopped her lunch tray down at Stephanie and Allie's table in the cafeteria. "Tell me something—" Darcy had said. "Is this food supposed to be our lunch? Or have I wandered into the science lab?"

Stephanie and Allie had burst out laughing. Stephanie still loved Darcy's off-the-wall sense of humor.

Now Darcy sat cross-legged on Stephanie's bed next to Allie. She reached up and twirled a lock of her bouncy black curls.

"Uh, Steph—couldn't you just put up your Do Not Enter sign?" Darcy asked.

"Yeah. Wouldn't that be simpler?" Allie added.

Stephanie was trying to push Michelle's night table in front of the chair.

Stephanie put a finger to her lips. She climbed onto her bed and motioned for her friends to lean in close.

"I told you, guys, this is top-secret stuff!"

"Are you afraid someone's going to break down your door to listen?" Allie asked.

"I'm just being extra careful," Stephanie told her. "I don't want anybody in my family to know the plan."

Stephanie reached over to the wall and took down the poster of Sheryl Crow, the pop singer. Underneath the poster was a large piece of construction paper covered with writing in different colors.

"You made charts?" Darcy asked in astonishment.

Allie's eyes widened. "Wow! This *is* big," she said. "What's going on, Steph?"

Stephanie grabbed her hair dryer and used it to point at the chart. "Listen closely. We are about to embark on a top-secret mission. You are to confide in absolutely no one, excluding the three people in this room. Are you with me so far?"

"I can't even understand you," Allie complained.

Stephanie pointed to the top of the chart. "Operation FUJG," she read. "It stands for Operation Fix Up Joey Gladstone."

Allie and Darcy exchanged surprised glances.

"You mean, you asked us here at nine o'clock on a Sunday morning . . . to find Joey a date?" Darcy asked.

"Exactly," Stephanie said. She swung the hair dryer in the direction of the chart. It flew out of her hand and crashed onto the floor.

Moments later there was a knock on the door. "Steph?" her dad called. "Are you okay?"

"Fine, Dad!" she answered. "Just dropped a book!"

"Okay, hon," Danny replied. The girls listened

as he walked away from the door and down the stairs.

Stephanie fell back on her pillow. "Whew! That was close!"

"Stephanie, don't you think you're getting a little carried away?" Allie asked.

"Maybe a little," she admitted. "But I have a good reason. I really really have to find somebody for Joey. He's been so sad lately. Last night I heard him call information to get the time. Then he asked the operator if she was seeing anyone! And it's all because Valentine's Day is just around the corner!"

"The operator? Whoa, that is weird. But why?" Darcy asked.

"Because Joey doesn't have a valentine! I know just how he feels. It's like this thing with me and Kyle. He—"

Darcy and Allie groaned at the mention of Kyle Sullivan's name.

"Steph! You promised you wouldn't drive us crazy about Kyle anymore!" Allie cried.

"And how can you compare Joey's situation to you and Kyle?" Darcy asked. "You've hardly said ten words to Kyle! We've told you a hundred times. Go talk to him. Go talk to him. Go talk to him. But do you? No!"

Stephanie winced. She *had* spoken to Kyle— once. She'd tried to ask if he was going to a football game. But the words got all jumbled as they flew out of her mouth. "Football, are you going to the Kyle game?" is what she actually said. She'd been trying to forget it ever since.

"Okay, okay!" Stephanie cried. "Forget Kyle. First we have to talk about Joey."

Stephanie pointed to the chart again. "In this column I've listed all Joey's qualities: His good looks, sense of humor, blah, blah, blah. Then in this column, I've listed all the qualities I think he needs in a woman: sensitivity, caring, good looks, funny, blah, blah, blah. Now, this little number in this column is my own personal rating system. A five is for 'very important' and a one is for 'not so important.' See? Next to caring I have a five. Important. Then here, next to 'nice car,' I have a one—not so important.

"So then, here, in this column, I've cross-listed all Joey's hobbies and numbered them with a second ratings system. So if you multiply . . ."

Darcy let out a phony snore. "Sorry, Steph,"

she apologized. "But your chart seems so . . . so . . ."

"Complicated," Allie finished for her.

Stephanie groaned, then tore the chart off the wall. "You're right," she admitted. "Okay, forget the chart." She leaned over to her night table and pulled a copy of *San Francisco Scene* out of the drawer. She tossed it onto the bed between them. "Here's the rest of my plan."

Stephanie quickly found the section she was looking for. She slapped the open pages with her hand.

"There!" she said.

Allie leaned over to read, then gazed at Stephanie in shock. "You're kidding!"

Darcy grabbed the magazine, then looked at Stephanie. "The personal ads?" she asked in amazement. "Have you lost your marbles?"

Stephanie hopped off her bed. "It's a great idea," she insisted. "Lots of people put ads in that section. They describe themselves and the person they'd like to meet. Then someone else reads the ad, they write to the magazine, and arrange a date. Then the two people meet and fall in love and get happily married!" Stephanie sneezed loudly as she finished.

Darcy and Allie stared at Stephanie in disbelief. "You *have* lost your marbles," Darcy said.

"Yeah, Steph," Allie agreed. "I mean, it can't be as easy as you make it sound."

"Well, I know that," Stephanie said, grabbing a tissue. "But I'm going to write such an excellent, romantic, hilarious, terrific ad for Joey that thousands of women will want to date him!"

"One problem," Allie pointed out.

"What's that?" Stephanie asked.

"Well, won't Joey be a little suspicious? Like, when your mailbox is overflowing with thousands of pink, perfumed envelopes addressed to him?"

Stephanie rubbed her chin. She hadn't thought about that.

She smiled suddenly. "That's easy. I won't use my return address. Then the letters won't come here," she explained. "What about it, Allie? Can I list your address? You're the first one who checks the mail in your house, right? And even if you're not, you could just tell your mom the letters are from a special pen pal project or something."

"Well, I'm not sure—" Allie began.

"But there's another problem, Miss Matchmaker," Darcy cut in, gazing at Stephanie. "How are you going to get Joey to go out with these women? He won't even know they wrote to him!"

"Oh. That *is* a problem," Stephanie admitted. She paced around the room awhile, then clapped her hands together. "Wait! I've got it! *I'll* arrange the dates! I'll decide on a place to meet each woman. Then I'll bring Joey there—and let the rest happen naturally."

Allie and Darcy exchanged doubtful looks.

"Please?" Stephanie pleaded. "For dear, wonderful, really miserable Joey?"

Allie sighed. "Yeah, okay. Since it's for Joey. But I still think it's a crazy idea!"

"Darce?" Stephanie asked. "Please?"

Darcy grinned and threw up her hands. "Why not?" she asked. "If it works, maybe we can find another boyfriend through the personal ads— for *me!*"

"And me!" Allie chimed in.

"Sure!" Stephanie laughed. Then she grew serious. "Though, if a personal ad doesn't work for you guys, there is something else you could try," Stephanie said.

"Now what are you talking about?" Allie asked.

"Another way to let someone you like know how you feel," she replied.

Darcy's eyes narrowed. "Does it involve charts?" she asked.

"No charts," Stephanie promised.

Darcy nodded. "Then let's hear it."

"Okay," Stephanie began. "Here's the deal. Joey and Uncle Jesse thought up a special Teen Romance Night for the radio station. You send in a special valentine message and they'll read it over the air."

"That *is* a great idea," Allie said, sounding interested.

"Just about perfect!" Darcy agreed.

"You mean, you guys want to do it?" Stephanie asked.

Allie shook her head. "No—*you* want to do it!"

"Me? Are you sure?" For a moment Stephanie felt sick to her stomach.

"It's perfect," Darcy exclaimed. "You write Kyle a terrific valentine—and have it read over the radio. He'll hear it and know how you feel."

"Darcy's right," Allie cried. "Go for it, Steph."

"It's foolproof," Darcy added. "And the best part of this plan is, you don't actually have to speak to Kyle."

Stephanie hesitated.

Allie and Darcy exchanged looks. "C'mon, Stephanie. It's a great idea," Darcy finally said. "That is, if you have the guts to go through with it. Do you?" she asked.

Stephanie looked serious. "I don't know," she admitted. "But I have two weeks to find out!"

CHAPTER
4

♦ ◢ ◆ ♦

Stephanie found some paper and a pen and the girls sat in a circle on the floor. Just as they were about to begin working on Joey's personal ad, there was a loud knock on the door.

"Stephanie! Let me in!"

Stephanie wrinkled her nose. "Michelle," she whispered.

"Stephanie!" Michelle cried again. "I want to get dressed! What's taking you so long?"

Stephanie leaned close to her friends. "I told her I was doing a science experiment for school this morning," she explained. "I said the bedroom can't have more than one person in it—or all the experimental data will be wrong!"

Allie held her hand over her mouth to stifle the giggles.

Stephanie cleared her throat. "Uh, Michelle, I'm not quite finished yet," she called out. "I need to complete testing the comparison of my data with the statistical information of—"

They heard Michelle groan from behind the door. "Oh, all right already!" she cried. "But you better be finished by lunchtime! I don't want to stay in my pajamas all day!"

When Michelle was gone, Stephanie picked up her pen again and began to write. She scribbled for a minute or so, then read what she'd written out loud.

" 'What light through yonder window breaks?' " she read. " 'It is the east and Juliet is the sun.' "

"Hey, that's good," Darcy remarked. "I don't know what it means, but it's good."

"Sounds very familiar," Allie said.

"Well, I didn't exactly write it," Stephanie admitted. "It's by Shakespeare."

Stephanie glanced over the ads in *San Francisco Scene.* In most of them, people pretty much described themselves. She figured she could start by trying to describe Joey. She wrote some more, then read out loud again.

"I'm cute, funny, sweet, and smart. I like hockey, funny movies, pizza, and Popeye."

Darcy laughed. "Good! Now say, 'looking for the perfect Olive Oyl'!"

"Yeah!" Stephanie added Darcy's suggestion and then some more on her own. When she was finished, she read the entire ad.

She cleared her throat. "Sleepless in San Francisco—that's the first line.."

"Oh, that's perfect!" Allie exclaimed. "*Sleepless in Seattle* was such a great movie!"

Darcy sighed dreamily. "Remember how that little boy tried so hard to fix his father up with Meg Ryan? And how he wants them to meet on top of the Empire State Building?"

That gave Stephanie a great idea. She could write in the ad that Joey would like to take his dream date somewhere romantic—like the top of the Empire State Building. She chewed on the pencil eraser and tried to think of a romantic place closer to home.

"I've got it!" Stephanie scribbled furiously on the paper. "Sleepless in San Francisco: 'What light through yonder window breaks? It is the east and

Juliet is the sun.' Me: Romeo/Tom Hanks/Popeye–type. I'm cute, funny, hunky, sweet, and smart. I like hockey, funny movies, pizza, and Betty Rubble. You: Juliet/Meg Ryan/Olive Oyl–type. If you are beautiful, sensitive, caring, smart, and like practical jokes, hockey, funny movies, pizza, Barney Rubble, and very big families, I would love to meet you in the middle of the Golden Gate Bridge. Signed, Lookin' for Love."

Allie and Darcy burst out laughing.

"Wow, I'd want to meet this guy!" Darcy joked.

"It's great, Steph!" Allie cried. "But why'd you put that in about big families?"

"Well, if Joey and his personal ad woman are going to date, she'll have to get used to big families. I thought I'd better mention it right up front."

Darcy stood. "Come on, let's call it in to the magazine."

Stephanie pulled the chair away from the door. Then she crept across the hall to her father's room. She checked to see if the coast was clear, then waved for Allie and Darcy to join her.

Stephanie dialed the number of the magazine and asked for the personal ads department. "It's a recorded message," she whispered. She listened for a few seconds. Then she groaned and hung up.

"Small problem," she told her friends.

"What?" Allie asked.

"The ads cost fifteen dollars," Stephanie began to explain.

"So?" interrupted Darcy. "Don't you have money saved up from your allowance? You must have fifteen dollars by now."

"Fifteen dollars a *line*," Stephanie added. "And there are how many lines?"

"Seven," Allie replied.

"That comes to one hundred and five dollars!" Darcy exclaimed.

Stephanie groaned. "Looks like it's back to the drawing board."

Darcy and Allie followed Stephanie back to her bedroom. They sat down on the floor while Stephanie scribbled some more. When Stephanie finally looked up, she didn't seem as happy as she had before.

"Okay, how about this?" she asked. "Me: cute, funny, and sweet. You: the same. Signed, Lookin' for Love."

Darcy and Allie sat quietly. Finally, Allie spoke. "It's okay," she said. "But it's nowhere near as great as the last one."

Stephanie sighed. "I know. But this one fits on one line."

Darcy shrugged. "I guess it will have to do, then. Come on, let's call it in."

Stephanie called the magazine a second time and read the ad into the tape recorder at the personal ads department. Then she left Allie's address for them to send the responses to. The recorded voice said the ad would appear the following Thursday.

The girls hurried downstairs to the kitchen to grab some lunch. They were munching on tuna sandwiches when Stephanie's uncle Jesse came in from his Sunday morning motorcycle ride. He hurried into the kitchen and took off his helmet.

Darcy looked up from her sandwich and burst out laughing. Immediately, Stephanie and Allie glanced up to see what was so funny. When they saw Jesse's hair, they cracked up too.

Jesse put his helmet on the table and stared at the girls. "What, may I ask, is so funny?"

Stephanie tried to swallow her sandwich and explain, but she was laughing too hard. She pointed to her uncle's head. "It's . . . your hair . . . it's . . ."

Jesse's eyes widened in horror. "My hair?" he

cried. "What's wrong with my hair?" He ran behind the kitchen counter and grabbed the toaster to check out his reflection.

"Sorry, Uncle Jesse." Stephanie tried to explain. "We've never seen you with helmet hair before."

"Ha, ha, ha." Jesse tried to fluff up his hair with his fingers. "You guys are a scream, you know that?"

"So, Uncle Jesse," Stephanie said, changing the subject, "about Teen Romance Night . . ."

"Hey! Did you decide to send a valentine?" Jesse asked. He put down the toaster and poured himself some iced tea.

"I think so," Stephanie replied. "But what exactly do I have to do?"

Jesse fluffed his hair some more. "Simple," he said. "Just write down your message and give it to Joey. He's in charge of making sure the valentines get to the deejay who's doing the show."

"Is there a line limit?" Stephanie asked.

"Huh?"

"Never mind."

"What about you two?" Jesse asked Allie and Darcy. "Want to let that certain someone know you care?" He winked at them.

Allie blushed. "Uh, I don't think so," she said.

34

"Sure, I do!" Darcy joked. "How about this—Dear Tom Cruise ..."

Everyone laughed. The door between the kitchen and the living room swung open and Michelle appeared in her pajamas. She stared angrily at her sister. "When did you finish your experiment?" she asked.

"Oh—a while ago," Stephanie admitted. "I guess it's safe for you to go up now."

Michelle spun away in a huff and marched upstairs.

"Experiment?" Jesse asked.

"It's a long story," Stephanie replied.

Jesse shrugged. "Well, if you guys decide to send a valentine, just let me or Joey know." He headed for the stairs, poufing his hair with each step.

When Jesse was gone, Allie took a swig of her iced tea. "So what's it going to be, Steph? Are you going to send Kyle a radio valentine or not?"

Stephanie took a bite of her sandwich. She chewed it for a long while.

That's a good question, she thought to herself. *Too bad I don't know the answer.*

CHAPTER
5

Thursday after school, Stephanie raced back home. She couldn't wait to see her personal ad in *San Francisco Scene* magazine. She found the mail lying on the coffee table with a copy of the magazine right on top. She flung her knapsack onto the floor, grabbed the magazine, and plopped down on the sofa.

Comet gazed at her from where he lay sprawled on the floor. Stephanie flipped to the personals section. Her finger scanned the ads.

"Here it is! 'Sleepless in San Francisco!' " she said excitedly. Comet raised his ears. "That's me! I mean us!" Stephanie told him. She grabbed the phone and dialed Allie.

"Hello?" a solemn voice answered.

"Allie, you sound terrible!" Stephanie cried. "What's wrong?"

"Everything." Allie groaned. "I just walked in the door and Aunt Wendy is crying her eyes out. She said she saw a car commercial that reminded her of Jimmy."

"Jimmy?"

"Her ex-boyfriend," Allie said. "It seems the color of the car in the commercial was the same color as Jimmy's eyes."

Stephanie rolled her own eyes. "You're kidding."

"No. Steph, you know, I hope I never fall in love."

"Allie! Don't say that! Of course you want to fall in love!"

"I don't know, Steph. You should see my once fun-loving, crazy, life-of-the-party aunt. She's sitting in her robe, sobbing over TV commercials and eating whipped cream straight from the can."

Stephanie laughed. "Is she that pathetic?" she asked.

"Totally," Allie replied. "And get this . . . my mom and dad are going to a medical convention in Anaheim—for a whole week! They're leaving me alone with her!"

Stephanie gasped. "Bummer!"

"You're telling me. What am I going to do? I don't think I can stand her alone for a whole week!"

"Hey! I have an idea," Stephanie said. "Why don't Darcy and I sleep over Saturday night?"

"That would be amazing. I'd be your best friend."

"Allie, you are my best friend," Stephanie pointed out.

"I know, but if you save me from this living nightmare, I'll be an even better friend!"

Stephanie laughed. "You've got a deal," she said. "Oh, wait! Don't hang up. Our ad came out today!" Stephanie opened the magazine. "Listen to this: Sleepless in San Francisco. Me: Cute, funny, and sweet. You: the same. Signed, Lookin' for Love."

Stephanie sighed. It wasn't the same without the Shakespeare and the Golden Gate Bridge. But maybe at least one nice woman would see it and reply.

"Listen, Al, I have to do some homework. I

have to pick a topic for my earth science project."

"Why don't you pick 'The Science of Staring at Kyle Sullivan'?" Allie suggested. "From what you tell us, that's all you do in that class anyway."

Stephanie laughed. Allie was right. She *did* spend an awful lot of time staring at Kyle in class. She'd stared at him so much, she could recognize the back of his head from thirty feet away.

"It's a major waste of a golden opportunity," Allie added. "You're so lucky that they combined your class with Kyle's for this project. I mean, they hardly ever put eighth and ninth graders together."

It was true, Stephanie realized. She *was* lucky to have this chance to be with Kyle. And all she'd ever done was stare at him. From a distance.

That's why it was important to pick a really good topic for this project. She really wanted to pick something that would impress Kyle.

"I'll come up with an idea tomorrow night, since I'm staying home again," Stephanie said.

"You are?" Allie asked. "But it's the weekend!"

"I know, but I've still got a little bit of a cold. And I'm worried about Joey. If I go out, who'll stop him from trying to date the operator again?"

Allie giggled.

"Anyway, I promised I'd baby-sit the twins. And it gives me time to work on my valentine to Kyle," Stephanie added.

"Read me what you have so far," Allie said.

"Okay. Dear Kyle . . ."

Allie waited a moment, then asked, "That's it? Come on, Stephanie, writing is your thing! This should be a cinch!"

Yeah, right, Stephanie thought to herself. *Trying to tell the most gorgeous guy in the world that I wish he were my valentine . . . when he doesn't even know I'm alive!*

A real cinch.

"Go fish, Cousin Stephanie, go fish!" Nicky bounced up and down and pointed to the pile of cards on the floor.

Stephanie picked a card. *Another Friday night*

with the twins, she thought. Oh, well, it was worth staying home to help Joey.

"Your turn, Joey," she said.

Joey barely looked up from the TV screen. He seemed really into the *Brady Bunch* rerun they were watching. Then Stephanie noticed he was actually staring into space instead of at the TV. *Poor Joey*, she thought.

Nicky reached over and grabbed Joey's head. He pointed it toward his handful of cards. "Your turn," he repeated.

"Sorry, kiddies. Okay. Alex, got any threes?"

Alex's face lit up in a smile. "No!" he shouted gleefully. "Go fish!"

Joey picked up a card just as Danny came downstairs.

Danny stood in front of the TV and modeled his latest outfit. "So? What do you think, guys?"

Stephanie gaped at the brightly colored sweatsuit her father was wearing. She put her face in her hands and shook her head. "Dad—"

"I know, I know," Danny said, grinning. "It's pretty wild, right? Marissa's a real health and fitness nut. So I went out yesterday and bought this jogging suit. I think Marissa might enjoy going Rollerblading tonight."

"Marvelous Marissa again," Stephanie mumbled under her breath.

Danny put his hands on his hips. "I asked you to stop calling her that," he scolded.

Stephanie smiled. "Sorry, Dad," she said. "It's just that you've talked about her so much all week. She can't be that incredible."

"Well, she is." Danny smiled from ear to ear. "I haven't asked her yet, but, boy, do I have a night of romance planned for Valentine's Day! First I'm going to pick her up in a limousine. Then I'm going to give her a box of candy and a dozen red roses."

Stephanie smiled. It was exactly how she imagined her Valentine's Day dream date with Kyle! She closed her eyes: She imagined herself listening to the radio. Suddenly her Valentine to Kyle came over the air. Moments later he was standing at her front door, carrying three dozen roses and a few boxes of chocolates. He pointed to a convertible sports car in the driveway and said . . .

". . . Danny Tanner, you are the most romantic man!" Her father's voice snapped her back to reality.

Stephanie noticed Joey's glum expression. She

glanced at her father and motioned for him to stop talking.

"Uh . . . and then we'll come right home," Danny finished awkwardly. "No big deal. It's only Valentine's Day, after all."

Joey sighed. "Easy for you to say," he complained. "You know you'll have a great date."

Jesse and Becky hurried into the room. "Hey, there's a car horn," Jesse said. "It must be Rob and Jodi Cabot."

"We're going out to dinner and a movie with them and the Sanderses," Becky explained. "It's Couples Night Out."

Danny smiled. "Wow, Couples Night Out. Now, that sounds—" He stopped when he noticed Stephanie motioning to Joey again.

"—really boring," he finished.

Jesse and Becky kissed the twins and rushed outside to meet their friends. "Thanks again, Steph!" they called out.

D.J. bounded down the stairs right after they left. "Did I hear a car horn?" she asked. "That must be my date."

Danny planted himself in front of the front door. "No, that was Jesse and Becky leaving," he said. "And you didn't tell me you were going out tonight."

"Yes, I did, Dad," D.J. replied. "With Ben."

"Who's Ben?" Danny asked.

D.J. laughed nervously. "Glen's twin brother."

Joey stared wide-eyed at D.J. "You're dating twins?" he asked. "Danny, is she allowed to do that? I mean, I can't even get *one* date!"

"I'm not dating Glen anymore," D.J. explained. "Things didn't exactly work out last weekend. He was cute, but a big bore. Then his twin brother asked me out. I figured it was my second chance."

Danny shook his head. "Well, drive safely and be home on time."

D.J. left and Stephanie went back to her game with the twins.

"Come on, Michelle!" Danny shouted up the stairs. "You'll be late for Joshua's!"

Joey looked up from his cards. "Maybe I'll have a girlfriend soon," he said. "Then we could have a Couples Night Out with Michelle and Joshua."

Stephanie laughed. At least Joey had made a joke again—even if it wasn't very funny. When her father and Michelle had gone, Stephanie played a few more rounds of Go Fish with the twins, then helped them to bed. Afterward, she joined Joey on the sofa to watch TV.

I'll try to get Joey's mind off dating, she thought to herself. She grabbed the remote control and channel-surfed. "What about this?" she asked Joey.

The TV showed an old black and white movie.

"Oh, Timothy!" a beautiful woman exclaimed. "I love you! I'm so glad you called! We'll never be lonely again!"

Stephanie gulped and hit the remote quickly. *No, no, no.* On another channel, a handsome man scooped up the baby and carried him over to a slim, pretty woman.

"Sabrina, isn't our family wonderful?" the man asked.

Whoops! Stephanie punched the remote again. The next channel showed four guys sitting in a restaurant. Then one guy leapt up from his chair. "At last! We were waiting for you!"

Four gorgeous women joined the guys at their table.

One of the women smiled. "This is the best Couples Night Out ever!" she said.

In a panic, Stephanie switched off the TV. "I've got a great idea," she said. "Let's bake cookies."

Stephanie grabbed Joey's hands and pulled

him into the kitchen. "Come on, Joey, we can have fun without dates!"

"You're right, Stephanie," Joey said. "I need to get my mind off women." He searched through the fridge for the cookie dough. "Maybe that's the trouble. Maybe I should just stay away from women and dating altogether. You know, that's not a bad idea." He stared at Stephanie. "I think you're really right, Steph."

"Wait a minute. I didn't say to do *that*," Stephanie protested.

"This is great," Joey went on. "No more of that 'Whatever you say, sweetheart,' and 'Whatever you want, dear.' And what about having to buy roses and rent limousines? It's cheaper to be single. Sure! That's the answer! No more dating for me. No siree."

"But it's really not all bad," Stephanie tried to tell him.

Joey ignored her. "You know, Steph, I'm feeling better already! I'm going to completely forget dating. I'll go out with my hockey buddies. See the old college crowd. Yup." He opened the package of cookie dough and started slicing.

"In fact," Joey continued, "I'll be happy if I never have another date again!"

Stephanie swallowed hard. *What about my personal ad?* she thought. *All those dates I was going to set up?* She watched as Joey arranged the sliced cookie dough on a tray and slipped it into the oven.

"Well, you don't have to go to such extremes—" she said.

"No, really, Stephanie. This is the answer. I'm tired of feeling sorry for myself. Moping around like that guy from that *Sleepless in Seattle* movie."

Stephanie gulped.

"Remember how everyone kept telling him he should go out and date? Well, he didn't need a date to cheer him up." Joey poured himself a tall glass of milk. "Just like me." Joey put an arm around Stephanie's shoulder. "I have my family and friends . . . and that's all I need!"

"But dating isn't *all* bad," Stephanie protested. "Take me and this guy from school, for instance. We—"

"Nope! I've made up my mind. This is it. From now on there'll be absolutely, positively no more dating!"

Stephanie groaned. *And I just blew two months' allowance on that ad!*

CHAPTER
6

◆ ◀ ◆ ◆

It was Saturday afternoon. Stephanie slid a slice of frozen pizza into the toaster oven. The telephone in the living room began to ring. She groaned loudly.

"Isn't anybody going to get that?" she shouted.

The phone rang again.

"Do I have to do everything around here?" She marched out of the kitchen and right past Joey, who sat on the sofa, reading the newspaper.

"Joey, don't you hear the telephone?" Stephanie asked.

Joey shrugged. "Yeah. But it isn't for me, so why answer?"

Stephanie shook her head. "Hello?" she answered. It was Allie. "Hi! What's up?" Stephanie greeted her. "I was going to call you after lunch. I was thinking, maybe we could go to the flea market today and look at some sneakers. My red canvas ones are pretty shot and I could really use some new ones. Maybe I'll try another color. What do you think of dark green? Or how about—"

"Stephanie! Will you stop talking for one second?" Allie sounded excited. "I have some news for you. About Operation FUJG!"

Stephanie gasped. "What? Tell me!" She turned away from Joey so he wouldn't overhear.

"Are you ready for this? About one minute ago a delivery man from *San Francisco Scene* delivered three sacks of mail to my house! And they're all for Lookin' for Love!"

"Get out of here!" Stephanie cried. "No way!"

"Way," Allie replied. "Three whole sacks! I'm not kidding. It's a good thing my parents are away. And Aunt Wendy was watching cartoons in the den. I had to drag those heavy things down to the family room by myself!"

"This is great!" Stephanie exclaimed a little too loudly.

"What's great?" Joey asked from the sofa.

Stephanie thought quickly. "Oh, uh, Allie finished a jigsaw puzzle."

Joey wrinkled his nose. "Why is that so great?"

"It was a really big puzzle," Stephanie said. "She's been working on it for years."

Joey shrugged and went back to his paper.

"So, anyway, Allie," Stephanie said loudly into the phone, "I can't wait to come over tonight—to see that really big jigsaw puzzle you just finished."

"Huh? What puzzle?" Allie asked.

"Yeah, I can't believe you finally finished it. What were there, like two hundred thousand pieces or something?"

"Stephanie, what are you talking about? Oh! Wait a sec! Joey's in the room with you, isn't he?"

"Bingo!" Stephanie said. "Okay, I'll be over around seven. Don't forget to call Darcy!"

She hung up the phone. Behind her, Joey flipped the pages of the paper and sighed. Stephanie gazed at him dreamily. This was so exciting! Joey sat there, totally unaware that his whole future was about to be decided for him.

Just imagine, Stephanie told herself. *A letter*

from Joey's soon-to-be sweetheart was waiting right now in one of those three mysterious sacks!

Stephanie raced down the steps into the Taylors' family room. When she saw the sacks of mail she let out a cry of surprise.

"Yikes! That's a lot of mail!" The sacks were bigger than she'd expected. A *lot* bigger.

Allie and Darcy were already sitting on the floor, surrounded by envelopes of all shapes and sizes.

"We tried to wait for you, Steph," Allie told her. "But we're dying to open these!"

"Yeah, this one was even sent overnight express from New York!" Darcy cried out.

"Really?" Stephanie plopped down next to them.

Darcy nodded. "There are a few from Los Angeles too."

"But most of them are from San Francisco and Oakland," Allie reported. She held up a really large envelope. "I wonder what's in this?"

"Open it," Stephanie commanded. She lowered her voice. "What did you tell your aunt we're doing down here?"

"I said we were working on a project for

51

school, and then you're both sleeping over," Allie said.

Stephanie felt a pang of guilt. Actually, she ought to be working on a topic for her earth science project. *But this is way more important,* she told herself. *Joey is family!*

Allie laughed. "Anyway, don't worry about Aunt Wendy," she said. "She rented a stack of movies for herself. She'll be upstairs crying her eyes out all night long."

"Excellent," Stephanie replied. "Now, let's get busy!" She ripped open the biggest envelope and peered inside. "Look at this picture!"

The girls crowded around. The photograph showed a woman in a formal gown. Her hair was pinned back tightly. She sat on a big chair as she sipped daintily from a teacup.

"Penelope Wainscott," Stephanie read from the back of the photo. "She looks so . . . serious. Definitely not Joey's type." She put the letter and photo off to the side. "This will be the No Way pile," she decided.

Darcy nodded eagerly. "And make another pile for the Maybes, and another for the Definite Maybes."

The girls began tearing through the letters.

But sorting them into piles was harder than they'd expected. Stephanie couldn't believe how many different types of women had written. There were letters from old women, young women, teachers, students, musicians, artists, actresses—even a construction worker! And they all sounded desperate to meet Lookin' for Love.

Allie lifted a letter. "I like this one," she said. "Her name is Risa. She says she's slim and attractive. She also says she writes—get this— comedy!"

Stephanie's eyes lit up. "Joey will love that!" A dreamy look spread over her face. "I can picture them together, making jokes nonstop."

Darcy shuddered. "Sounds awful to me."

"But you're not Joey," Stephanie pointed out. "That's why this is so hard. We have to ignore our own feelings and choose the letters that Joey would like."

"Well, I say Risa is a definite," Allie said.

Stephanie agreed. Next, Darcy held up a letter. "Listen to this one," she said. "Hello, Lookin' for Love. I am Natasha. I am dancer. I am friendly. I would much like to make arrangements to meet you."

Stephanie giggled. "Where is she from?" she asked.

Darcy glanced at the letter. "Well, she lives in San Francisco now," she said. "But she sounds really foreign and exotic, doesn't she?" Darcy read some more. "A dancer!" she cried in excitement. "I'll bet she's a Russian ballerina!"

Stephanie smiled. "That would be excellent." She imagined Natasha onstage at the Civic Center, dancing *Swan Lake* in front of hundreds of people. Joey gazes at Natasha from his special seat near the stage. His eyes meet her dark ones . . . he blows a kiss. . . .

"This is so romantic! I'll bet Natasha is tall and thin and beautiful." Stephanie sighed.

"And graceful," Allie added. "Remember my old ballet instructor, Miss Maxina? She was from Russia. And she was gorgeous!"

Darcy nodded. "Natasha is a Definite."

They put Natasha's letter in the Definite pile. Stephanie yawned loudly. "Only two definites so far! What time is it?"

Allie glanced at her watch. "Ten-thirty!" she exclaimed, rubbing her eyes. "How did it get so late?"

"And when should we stop?" Darcy wondered.

"We can't stop until we have at least five Definites," Stephanie decided. "Or until we've gone through all three mail sacks," she added. "Whichever comes first." With a grim expression, she ripped open another envelope.

Darcy groaned, staring at the mountains of mail in front of them. "Have a heart, Steph," she begged. "It'll take forever to go through all this."

"She's right," Allie quickly agreed. "At this rate we'll never find five Definites."

"You're wrong," Stephanie cried. "But don't worry. This one isn't a definite. It's a *Perfect!*"

CHAPTER
7

◆ ◀ ◆ ◆

Stephanie cleared her throat and read. "Dear Lookin' for Love. All my life I have been waiting for someone like you. Somebody sweet, caring, and fun. It took me many years of hard work to get through medical school. But now I am an accomplished physician, and searching for somebody to share my life. After reading your letter, I believe I have finally found you. Please call. Signed, Dr. Lee Gatsby."

"Wow! That is *so* romantic!" Allie cried.

"And she sounds so sincere," Darcy added.

"And it would really be great to have a doctor

in the family," Stephanie agreed. "Someone in my house is always getting sick or breaking something."

Stephanie placed Dr. Gatsby's letter on top of the Definite pile.

"Great!" Allie said. "Because one Perfect and two Definites must equal five Definites. Right?" she asked.

"Wrong," Stephanie told her. Darcy and Allie both groaned.

"At least let us take a break," Darcy pleaded.

Stephanie agreed to that. They hurried upstairs, thankful to stretch their legs. Aunt Wendy was collapsed on the sofa, weeping into a crumpled tissue. They had to tiptoe past her to get into the kitchen.

Allie was pouring three glasses of milk when Aunt Wendy burst into the room.

"Oh!" she said, startled. "Hi, guys. I didn't see you come in here." She pulled her bathrobe tighter around her waist and tried to neaten her tangled hair.

"Aunt Wendy, you remember Stephanie," Allie said politely.

Stephanie smiled at Allie's aunt. "Hi."

"And this is Darcy Powell."

"Hi, Stephanie. Hi, Darcy," Wendy said. "Uh, excuse my appearance. I'm just . . . uh, well . . ."

"Don't worry about us," Stephanie said, trying to make her feel better. "You don't have to dress up when we're around. I mean, it's not like we're your dates or—oops!" Stephanie clapped her hands over her mouth.

"That's okay, Stephanie," Aunt Wendy said. "Do you have a boyfriend yet?"

Stephanie's eyes widened. "Well, I—"

"I sure hope not," Aunt Wendy went on without waiting for Stephanie to finish. "Men! They're nothing but trouble!"

"Well, there is this one really cute guy—" Stephanie began.

"Forget him!" Aunt Wendy exploded. "Trust me, girls, they're not worth it. They'll only break your heart! They'll borrow your CDs and never return them. Or they'll forget to feed your fish. Or they'll call off the wedding one month before the big day, even though everything's already paid for and—" Aunt Wendy began crying again.

"We'd better go," Allie whispered to her friends. "Uh, sorry, Aunt Wendy," she said in a louder voice, "but we really have to get back to our project."

Allie's aunt wiped her eyes and blew her nose loudly. "Oh, I'm sorry. I didn't mean to go on like that. Nice to see you again, Stephanie. Bye, Darcy."

The three girls hurried downstairs.

"Boy, your aunt Wendy *does* look awful," Stephanie whispered to Allie.

Allie nodded. "I told you! She hasn't changed out of that robe in three days!"

"Yuck!" Darcy whispered.

Stephanie glanced at all the letters still to be opened. It was nearly midnight. And she was really tired. But then she thought of Joey. *It has to be done,* she told herself firmly. *Even if we have to stay up all night.*

Another hour passed and they hadn't added anything to the Definite pile.

Suddenly Darcy started giggling. She waved a letter in the air. "I *love* this," she cried. "Listen: 'Hey! I'm the one. Call me.' "

Stephanie and Allie waited to hear more.

"That's all?" Stephanie asked.

Darcy laughed. "Yeah—short and to the point. She signs it, Lookin' for Love Too."

"That's cute," Allie agreed. *"Now* can we go to sleep?"

"No! We don't know anything about her," Stephanie pointed out.

"Maybe not," Darcy said. "But at least this letter is different. Not like all these long, boring letters that tell you everything from what shampoo they use to what they ate for breakfast."

Darcy was right. Most of the letters were big snoozers. And Joey liked things snappy. When he and Jesse did their radio show, he was always saying, "Keep it short, Jesse. Short and snappy!"

"Okay," Stephanie agreed. " 'Short and snappy' to the Definite pile."

"Excellent!" Darcy cried. "That means we're almost finished. One more Definite and we can go to sleep—at last!"

"And this is it!" Stephanie cried a few minutes later. "A Definite if I ever saw one!"

Allie and Darcy both groaned in relief.

Stephanie read out loud: "I'm five foot four, with brown hair and blah, blah, blah ... Okay, here's the good part! 'I'm a chemistry professor and I play ice hockey and love Italian food!' "

She gazed at Darcy and Allie. "Isn't that terrific?"

Darcy stared at her blankly. "I don't get it," she said. "Why is she a Definite?"

"I don't get it either," Allie said.

"Oh! I forgot you weren't there." Stephanie giggled. "You see, the other night D.J. had a date with someone from her chemistry class. And Joey said he wished *he* had a date with someone in his chemistry class. Then my dad said, 'Joey, you don't *have* a chemistry class,' and Joey said—"

Darcy held her arm out. "Okay! Okay! We get the picture!"

Stephanie looked at her watch. "One-thirty." She yawned. "Thank goodness we're finished for the night!"

"Yahoo!" Allie cheered. "Finally—we get some sleep."

They opened the queen-sized sofa bed and climbed under the covers.

"Now all we have to do is get up early tomorrow and write down answers to these five women. Then we'll call the special message center at the magazine and leave the time and place they should meet Joey. Hey, Al, how's your phone voice?" Stephanie asked.

Allie yawned loudly. "Not bad," she answered.

"Good," Stephanie said. "Because you can pretend to be Joey's secretary when we call. Okay?"

"Sure," Allie agreed. "Now can we go to sleep, please?"

"Uh-huh." Stephanie closed her eyes and snuggled against her pillow.

It felt great to have gotten so much good work done. Thanks to her and Darcy and Allie, Joey was on his way to having a perfect Valentine's Day. Now, if only she could say the same for herself!

CHAPTER
8

◆ ◀ ◼ ◆

On Monday afternoon Stephanie sat across from Allie and Darcy at a big table. The three of them had chosen to take study hall in the library this semester. It was a great chance to hang out together during the day—which was helpful in times of crisis. And right then, at that moment, Stephanie was having a major crisis: She couldn't finish her valentine to Kyle.

Stephanie kicked Darcy's leg under the table.

"Hey!" Darcy whispered loudly. "What was that for?"

"Sorry, Darce," Stephanie whispered back.

"But I waited three whole minutes for you to look up. I had to get your attention somehow!"

Stephanie kept her voice down so Mr. Miller, the librarian, wouldn't hear. No one was supposed to talk during study hall, and Mr. Miller was very strict.

Darcy rubbed her shin. "So, what do you want?" she asked. "I have to read this story before next period."

Mr. Miller was standing nearby at the card catalogue. He cleared his throat extra loudly. When Stephanie looked up, he raised his finger to his lips.

"Sorry." Stephanie mouthed the word. She glanced down at her earth science textbook and pretended to read. She really *should* have been reading—she still needed a topic for her big earth science project.

But when Mr. Miller turned back to the card catalogue, she kicked Darcy in the leg again. Very gently this time.

"What?" Darcy whispered. Allie looked up too. She had been punching numbers on her calculator at an incredibly fast pace. "Is this something important?" she whispered.

"Extremely. I need help!" Stephanie cried.

"It's this valentine for Kyle. I've written about fifteen versions. All of them were terrible. This is the latest one, and it's just not right."

Darcy carefully marked the place in her book. She and Allie leaned closer to Stephanie. "You'd better read us the latest one."

Stephanie reached into the pages of her earth science text and pulled out a piece of notebook paper.

"You did get further than 'Dear Kyle,' didn't you?" Allie whispered with a giggle.

Stephanie made a face. "Yes, I have." She read from the piece of paper. "To Kyle Sullivan. Red are the roses, green is the grass. You have an admirer in your joint-eighth-and-ninth-grade earth science class."

Allie laughed—a little too loudly. Mr. Miller started walking toward their table. There was an impatient look on his face.

Uh-oh! Stephanie buried her nose in her textbook. On either side of her, Darcy and Allie did the same. Luckily, Reena Prince suddenly raised her hand at her table across the room.

"Mr. Miller," Reena called. "I don't know how to find the reference book I need. Can you help me?" Mr. Miller shot a warning glance toward Stephanie's table, then hurried to Reena's side.

"Whew. That was a close one!" Stephanie pushed the valentine poem into the center of the table again.

Darcy leaned over and scowled at it. "The first part is great. The ending's wrong. Too long, maybe?"

Stephanie crossed out 'joint-eighth-and-ninth-grade' and read the poem over to herself. It sounded much better.

"Thanks," she told Darcy. "It did help to make it shorter. But do you think it's too corny?"

Darcy shook her head. "I think it's fine."

Stephanie sighed. "Good. That leaves only one tiny, minor problem." She took a deep breath. "There are lots of girls in our class. How will Kyle know it's from me?"

Darcy and Allie exchanged impatient glances. "Because it'll be signed Stephanie Tanner," Darcy answered.

Stephanie frowned and chewed on her pen cap. "I don't know about that. Once this gets read over the radio, my secret crush won't be a secret anymore. I'm not sure I'm ready for that step."

Allie sighed. "Fine. Then don't sign it," she said. "But you'll ruin everything."

"How?" Stephanie demanded.

"Because if you don't sign it, Kyle might think the valentine is from someone else. Then, even if he likes you, he might not want to admit it. Not without knowing that you like him first." Allie crossed her arms over her chest.

"That could happen," Stephanie agreed.

"I disagree," Darcy stated. "You *shouldn't* sign it, Steph. What if Kyle *doesn't* like you the same way? You'll be all embarrassed. If you don't sign it, it won't matter if Kyle doesn't like you. Because you can always say it was from someone else."

Stephanie frowned. Talking about Kyle *not* liking her made her more nervous than ever.

"Wait. Let me get this straight," Stephanie said. "I'm not signing it?"

"Right!" Darcy said.

"Wrong!" Allie cried. "If he doesn't know it's from you, then why send it in the first place? You're just being chicken again!"

Stephanie groaned and dropped her head onto the table. She thought a bit, then scribbled on her notebook paper. "What if I send it like this?"

she asked. "To Kyle Sullivan: Red are the roses, green is the grass, you have an admirer in your earth science class. If you know who I am, leave me a note in my locker.' That way, if there's a note in my locker from Kyle, I'll—"

Allie and Darcy motioned frantically at her to be quiet.

Stephanie frowned. Was Mr. Miller coming back to their table? She spun around in her seat to look—and nearly choked. *Oh, no! I don't believe this!*

It wasn't Mr. Miller. It was Kyle Sullivan.

He was standing less than two feet away. His back was to Stephanie as he searched through the bookshelf. But he was close enough to have heard everything!

I'll die if he heard me say his name, Stephanie thought. *Please, say he didn't hear me!*

Stephanie whirled back around—and knocked a book off the table. It clattered loudly to the floor. She felt her face flush and covered it with her hands.

This can't be happening!

Stephanie heard someone come up behind her. She turned again, very slowly this time. She gulped. Kyle stood right by her chair. In his hand was the book she had dropped.

"This yours?" He held it out to her.

"Huh? Er . . . uh-huh," she managed to say. *Stop staring at him!* she scolded herself. But she couldn't help it. He was so cute! And she never had been so close to him before.

"Steph!" Darcy hissed. "Take the book!"

Stephanie grabbed the book from Kyle. He smiled and went back to searching the bookshelves.

Smooth, Stephanie. "Huh. Er . . . uh-huh." Real smooth! She groaned out loud. Her big chance to talk to Kyle—and she'd uttered four dumb syllables!

"You should see your face." Allie gave her a sympathetic smile.

Darcy stared at Stephanie impatiently. "Why didn't you say hi? Or thank him for picking up your book? Or anything?"

Stephanie swallowed hard, then found her voice. "I couldn't!" she cried. "I'm so embarrassed I could die! What's he doing now?"

Darcy gazed over Stephanie's head. "He—"

"Don't let him see you looking!" Stephanie interrupted.

"Get a grip, Steph." Darcy laughed. "He's not even looking over here. He found what he wanted on the shelves, and he already walked away."

Stephanie dropped her head back down on the table.

"Uh, Stephanie?" Allie whispered. "I think, maybe you're not quite ready to sign that valentine."

"I think Allie's right," Darcy agreed.

Stephanie groaned.

"It's okay," Allie assured her. "Stick to your strong points. You're a good writer. So think about what report to write for your science project. Does it have to be about ecology? Or can it be about some other kind of science, like astronomy maybe, or even chemistry—"

"Chemistry!" Stephanie cried. She bolted upright in her chair. Mr. Miller glanced her way and Stephanie clapped both hands over her mouth.

Chemistry! She had nearly forgotten! Tonight was the night of Joey's first date—with the chemistry teacher!

Stephanie, Allie, and Darcy had made careful

arrangements with the one Perfect and four Definites on their date list. Allie had made the calls to set up a time and place for Joey to meet each woman. The chemistry teacher was date number one. She'd already left her reply with the message center, saying that she'd be glad to meet Joey that night. She was supposed to show up at their house right after dinner. Stephanie shifted uncomfortably in her chair.

Operation FUJG had all sounded like a great idea. But now that it was about to start, Stephanie wasn't so sure. She still had no idea how she would actually get Joey to go out with this woman. Stephanie glanced at her watch and groaned again. In exactly five and a half hours Operation FUJG would begin. And she wasn't in the least bit ready!

CHAPTER
9

◆ ◥ ◆ ◆

Stephanie paced the length of her bedroom. It was almost time for dinner, and she still had no idea how to handle Joey's surprise date.

"You're going to wear a hole in the floor," Michelle said as Stephanie crossed the room for the sixteenth time.

Stephanie ignored her and glanced at her alarm clock. Only two more hours! This was no time for arguments with her little sister. This wasn't even the time to worry about the way she'd embarrassed herself in the library with Kyle.

In exactly two hours a pretty brunette chemistry teacher was going to show up in their living room. And she would expect to meet Joey. And go out with him.

Stephanie gulped. *I could make it seem like a coincidence,* she told herself. *As if she's dropped by for some other reason and just happens to meet Joey.* How in the world was she going to do that? Pretend she'd signed Joey up for adult chemistry classes?

Soon it was dinnertime, and Stephanie still hadn't come up with a single idea. She and Michelle hurried into the kitchen. It was their turn to set out the food. Her dad and Uncle Jesse were already there, putting finishing touches on the meal.

"Steph, honey—would you carry the turkey to the table?" Her father opened the oven door and waved a potholder in her direction.

Stephanie lifted the big roasting pan out of the oven and set the turkey on a serving platter. She carried it carefully to the table.

"By the way, Dad," she asked, trying to seem casual, "have you seen Joey tonight?"

"Joey?" Danny gazed absently around the kitchen.

Stephanie frowned. Her dad was acting strangely. "Here's Joey," Michelle said.

Joey bounded into the kitchen. Stephanie took one look at him and cringed in horror.

"Joey!" she cried. "Tell me that's *not* what you're wearing to dinner!"

Joey had on his oldest pair of faded, ripped jeans. And with them he wore the top from his Bullwinkle pajamas. As if that weren't bad enough, his hair was sticking out in every direction and his face was covered with stubble. It looked as if he hadn't shaved in days.

"What's the big deal?" Joey raked his fingers through his messy hair. "It's not like we're expecting some movie star for dinner. Are we?"

"Uh, no, not exactly, but—" Stephanie stopped. She couldn't tell him who they *were* expecting.

Joey glanced down. "Anyway, this is a clean pajama top," he said. He took his seat at the table and tucked a napkin into his pajama collar.

"I think he looks cool," Michelle said. "Bullwinkle is so cute."

Stephanie glared at Michelle. She thrust the bowl of potatoes at her. "You carry this. I'll take the asparagus," she said.

74

Stephanie's stomach flip-flopped. Things just couldn't get worse. She'd been so worried about getting Joey to go out with the teacher. Now she had a new worry. How could she possibly force a good-looking, intelligent teacher to go out with Joey?

Uncle Jesse slapped Joey's shoulder. "Don't listen to Stephanie, old buddy. You look fine. As long as you're comfortable."

"Thanks, Jess," Joey mumbled.

"Don't mention it. But since you're obviously not wearing it—could I borrow your best leather jacket tonight?"

"You mean Ricardo?" Joey asked.

Stephanie raised her eyebrows. "You named your jacket?"

"It's not just a jacket," Joey explained. "It's the coolest thing I own. In college I was a chick magnet in that thing!"

"Well, how about it, then?" Jesse asked. "It's not like you have a date or anything."

Joey's face fell.

Jesse winced. "Whoops, sorry. I didn't mean it to come out that way."

Joey shrugged. "You're right. I don't need it. You go ahead. Have a great night with Ricardo."

"Who's Ricardo?" Becky asked as she entered the kitchen. She led Nicky by the hand to his high chair. D.J. followed, holding Alex.

"Ricardo is Joey's jacket," Michelle explained. "Joey is letting Uncle Jesse wear it so Uncle Jesse can be the chicken magnet."

Becky stared at Michelle in confusion. "The what?"

Michelle opened her mouth to answer, but Jesse clapped his hand over it. "We were discussing how Joey could meet a nice woman."

Joey looked up. "We were?"

Jesse nodded. "Sure. And I have the perfect idea. Learn to play the guitar! Women love it."

"That's ridiculous, Jesse," Becky said. "First of all, it takes years to learn how to play the guitar. And secondly—"

"A cruise is a better idea," D.J. finished. "People fall in love on cruises all the time."

"Or at a singles dance," Becky said. "I went to a few nice ones before I met Jesse."

Michelle ducked out from Jesse's grip. "My teacher met her husband at the dog run near Hollow Park," she said. "You could take Comet there, Joey."

"I don't know, Michelle—" Joey began.

"What do you think, Dad?" D.J. asked. "How should Joey meet the woman of his dreams?"

Stephanie held her breath. She didn't know what she'd do if her dad—or anyone—suggested the personal ads. But Danny didn't even answer. He was staring into space, smiling.

"Dad?" D.J. repeated. "Hello! What planet are you on today?"

Danny turned red. "Sorry, guys. I was just thinking about a great conversation Marissa and I had yesterday. Let me tell you exactly what she said—"

"Marvelous Marissa again!" Stephanie shook her head. "Dad, you can't possibly remember every word she said."

Danny laughed. "No, of course not." He reached into his pocket and pulled out a tiny tape recorder. "I have it all on tape."

"Dad, you're amazing!" D.J. said with a laugh. "You had only two dates with her."

"I know, I know. It's just that Marissa is incredible. And I think . . . I think she may be *the* one!"

"I'm glad you found someone special," Joey said. "That's terrific—if you like that sort of thing."

"What 'thing'?" Danny asked.

"Dating," Joey said seriously. "Now, I prefer the life of a single guy. There's no one to answer to. No one to tell you you can't watch sports. No one to say you can't put your feet on the coffee table."

"You put your feet on my new coffee table?" Danny asked.

"You're missing the point," Joey told him. "I'm trying to say that dating isn't for me. Not anymore. Nope, this is one swinging dude who's given up dating. And it was all Stephanie's idea."

Eight pairs of eyes stared at Stephanie. She slumped in her chair.

"Yessir," Joey said. "I'll be happy if I don't talk to a woman for the next six months!"

"Hey!" Becky, D.J., and Michelle said in unison.

"Oh, I didn't mean you guys. I meant, no *new* women. This dude is on permanent dating vacation. No fix-ups for me. Not now. Never."

Stephanie dropped her head into her hands. *That's just great. And what am I going to tell the five women I've lined up for Joey to meet this week?*

Not to mention the chemistry teacher who'll be here in about five minutes!

Stephanie couldn't think straight with so many people around. She'd have to come up with a plan as soon as dinner was over. But the doorbell rang just as she was placing an armful of dirty dishes into the sink. She felt her heart drop into her stomach.

She raced into the living room. Joey was already at the front door.

"Yes . . . ?" Joey asked. Stephanie saw a young woman peer at him through the open door. She was staring at Joey's Bullwinkle pajama top.

"Uh, are you 'Lookin for . . .'" the woman began to say.

Stephanie leapt across the room and pushed Joey out of the way.

"A housekeeper?" she cried. "Oh, no, we don't need one! But thanks for asking. It's been a pleasure meeting you. Bye now!"

"But—" the woman protested.

"No thank you!" Stephanie slammed the door in the woman's face.

Whew! she thought. *That was too close!*

She spun around to go back into the kitchen.

To her surprise, her entire family was standing in front of her.

"Stephanie, why did you do that?" Joey asked. "You closed the door right in that woman's face!"

"What's going on, Stephanie?" her father demanded.

Stephanie bit her bottom lip. She blinked innocently. "Oh, uh, she was just some saleslady. Selling . . . uh, encyclopedias. And we already have one! She was here earlier and I told her no thanks. Some people are *too* pushy, aren't they?"

She hurried back to the kitchen. Date number one was a total disaster. And if Joey didn't change his mind about dating, how would she ever get him to go out with dream date number two?

CHAPTER
10

♦ ◀ ◾ ♦

"Darcy, what do you think about that idea?"

Stephanie watched as Darcy tapped the cafeteria table with her fingers. Then she started to sing. Stephanie reached over and snapped off Darcy's Walkman.

"Darcy!" Stephanie exclaimed. "Did you hear anything we said?"

"Sure," Darcy replied uneasily. "You, uh, were talking about Joey and his second blind date. Right?"

Stephanie made a face. "So you didn't hear Allie's idea."

Darcy shook her head.

"For those of us who weren't paying attention, Allie had a good idea," Stephanie said. "Allie thinks I should get Joey as close to the meeting place as possible. Then at the last second I make up a story and drag him inside—to meet the woman of his dreams."

"Everything else is all set," Allie explained. "Steph and Joey will be home tonight. Everyone else in her family has plans. So all we need is a good reason for Joey to leave the house."

"Where did you arrange to meet date number two?" Darcy asked.

"Perk Up," Stephanie replied.

"A coffee bar?" Darcy asked. "You don't drink coffee."

"I know. That's the problem," Stephanie pointed out. "It's a really popular place. Great for a first date. But I can't ask Joey to take *me* out for coffee. I need a cover story. You know— an excuse to get him there."

"Got it!" Darcy cried. "There's a drugstore right next to Perk Up. You could pretend your cold is much worse. Then ask Joey to take you to the drugstore for cold medicine! He can't say no to that."

"You're a genius," Stephanie said. "That's a great idea!"

Allie nodded eagerly. "Yeah, you could pretend you're so weak and dizzy that you're about to faint. Really ham it up."

Stephanie grinned. "Count on me to do that!" she joked. "When it comes to acting, I'm a natural. They don't call me Jodie Foster for nothing!"

Darcy narrowed her eyes. "They don't call you Jodie Foster."

"I know, Darcy, it's just an expression! Now, turn up the volume on that Walkman—I feel like dancing!"

"But aren't you coming down with a cold?" Allie asked jokingly.

Stephanie grinned as she did a little dance. She suddenly clutched her throat. In the scratchiest voice she could muster, she cried, "Medicine! Quick! I need some strong medicine!"

Suddenly there was a hand on Stephanie's shoulder. Still holding her throat, she spun around—and found herself staring at Kyle Sullivan. His brown eyes were filled with concern.

"Are you okay?" Kyle asked.

Stephanie felt her cheeks burning. *Don't just*

stand there staring again! she told herself. *Say something!*

"Uh, yeah," she croaked in her scratchy voice. She cleared her throat. "I mean, yes, I'm fine. I was, uh, just goofing around." *Not too clever,* she thought. *But at least I managed more than four syllables.*

Kyle laughed. "You're some actress!" He pushed his wavy blond hair away from his eyes. "I was about to run for the school nurse!"

Stephanie laughed. And shot an "I told you so" look at her friends.

"Anyway," Kyle said, "I'm glad you're not sick. I've been looking all over school for you."

Stephanie's jaw dropped open. Oops! She quickly shut her mouth. "You . . . you have?" she asked. She was so nervous, her voice got higher and higher. "I mean, you were? I mean, why?"

"Well, you know that project we're supposed to do for earth science?"

Stephanie nodded.

"Didn't I hear you say something to Ms. Altman about the rain forest?"

Stephanie's mind was a blank. Then she remembered asking the teacher if she could write about ecology in the rain forest. It wasn't much of an idea yet.

"Well," Kyle continued, "I thought maybe we could make a model of a rain forest. That is, if you want a partner."

Stephanie tried to keep her jaw up this time, but it was hard work. She couldn't believe her ears! Kyle Sullivan actually wanted to be partners with her!

"Definitely!" she squeaked.

Great, Steph. If your voice goes any higher, he'll think you communicate only with dogs.

She lowered her voice. "Of course. Making a model would be great!"

Kyle smiled. "Excellent. I'll tell Ms. Altman. We could get together next week or something. I have some really cool ideas for this project. My brother's been to a rain forest and he took lots of photos."

Stephanie hadn't heard a word Kyle said after "we'll get together next week." But she realized he had finished talking, so she smiled brightly. A few seconds passed in silence. Stephanie desperately tried to think of something else to talk about so he wouldn't leave.

"Are you a Kings fan?" she suddenly blurted out, pointing to his L.A. Kings hockey shirt.

Kyle grinned. "Huge fan."

"My dad's friend Joey interviewed Wayne Gretzky on his radio show once," Stephanie told him.

"Joey Gladstone is a friend of your dad's?" Kyle seemed impressed.

Stephanie smiled. "Actually, Joey's my friend too."

"Excellent," Kyle said. "I listen to him all the time. *Rush Hour Renegades* is my favorite show. I like Jesse too."

"Jesse's my uncle," Stephanie said.

Now Kyle seemed really impressed. "That is so cool!"

The bell rang for their next class. Stephanie felt a rush of disappointment. She didn't want Kyle to leave. She could have stayed in the lunchroom talking to him forever.

"I've got to go," Kyle said. "See you later, okay?"

Stephanie smiled. Kyle waved to Allie and Darcy, then left the cafeteria. The instant he was gone, Stephanie collapsed onto her chair. She was in a state of total shock.

"Did that really just happen?" she cried.

"Yes! And it was totally fabulous!" Darcy wrapped an arm around Stephanie's shoulders.

"Wow!" was all Allie could say.

"And you thought he didn't know who you were!" Darcy laughed.

Stephanie was in a trance. She stared at the cafeteria doors where Kyle had disappeared. "Pinch me, I must be dreaming," she said to her friends.

Darcy pinched her on the shoulder.

"Ow!" Stephanie cried. "Well, I'm awake all right. Then it really happened." She sighed dreamily. "Me. Stephanie Tanner. Kyle Sullivan wants me to be his partner! Did you guys hear every word?"

"Yup," Darcy said.

"Did you hear the part about how he was looking for me?"

"Heard it," Allie told her.

"And when he said we should get together next—"

"We heard it!" Darcy cried. "We were sitting two feet away!"

The bell rang again. Allie leapt up. "It all really, truly, positively, absolutely happened. I'm marking it on my calendar right now." She waved an imaginary pen in the air. "Wednesday, February eleventh. Kyle Sullivan spoke to Stephanie Tanner. Now, come on! We'll all be late to class."

Stephanie motioned for her friends to go ahead without her. She couldn't move. Not for the next few minutes anyway. For now all she could do was sit in her chair and replay her conversation with Kyle. Over and over again.

CHAPTER
11

◆ ◀ ◂ ◆

Stephanie waited until seven-thirty that evening before knocking on Joey's door. She waited for him to answer.

She was positive that dream date number two was going to go perfectly. Natasha and Joey were really going to hit it off. They had to. After her incredible chat with Kyle that afternoon, what could possibly go wrong? This was obviously a wonderful day for romance!

Stephanie stared into space, imagining Joey and Natasha together. She could see their entire romance, ending with a big, beautiful wedding.

Joey would be dapper in a tuxedo and sneakers. And Natasha would be tall and beautiful in a white wedding gown and toe shoes.

Stephanie was there too, of course. She looked gorgeous in a satiny peach bridesmaid gown. Kyle was at her side, looking amazingly handsome in a pale gray suit.

Then, somehow, it was her own wedding she was dreaming about. She and Kyle were walking down the aisle in the school cafeteria . . . Allie and Darcy were throwing rice . . .

"I said, who is it?" Joey repeated loudly.

Stephanie nearly jumped. "Uh, Joey, it's me!"

"What do you want, Steph? I'm listening to a big game."

"I, uh, I need a ride to the drugstore," Stephanie called. "Can you take me?"

"Can't Danny take you?" Joey called back.

"He's working tonight," Stephanie replied.

"What about D.J.?"

"Library."

"Jesse?"

"Supermarket. With Becky and the twins and Michelle. Joey! Please!" Stephanie cried. "It's important! I—I really don't feel so well."

She heard Joey rush to the door. *So far so good.*

Her smile turned into a frown when Joey emerged from his room. He was wearing a beat-up, faded green sweatsuit that looked about fifty years old.

"Is that what you're wearing?" Stephanie asked.

Joey gazed at his clothes. "Yeah, what's the matter with it?"

Stephanie curled her lip. "It's sort of grungy, don't you think?"

"Stephanie, you need to go to the drugstore! What difference does it make how I look?"

"Well, can you at least brush your hair?" Stephanie asked. "I mean, I would hate people to think we were slobs. I do have a reputation to uphold, you know."

Joey grumbled but stopped to brush his hair. He even threw a light jacket over his clothes before hurrying to the car.

On the way to the drugstore, Joey flipped on the radio. A love song came on. He changed stations. Another love song. He changed stations again. At the sound of the third love song, he reached out and snapped off the radio. Luckily, they reached the drugstore quickly. Stephanie glanced at her watch. It was ten minutes to eight. Natasha would meet them next door at eight.

Joey followed Stephanie to the cold-medicine section. "How are you feeling?" he asked in an anxious voice.

"Worse," she croaked. She scanned the rows and rows of pills and syrups. She lifted a few and pretended to read their labels.

"Steph, come on already. You're looking worse by the minute."

Stephanie sneaked another peek at her watch. Five minutes to go! Suddenly she grabbed the display shelf and swayed back and forth. "Ooh," she moaned.

"Stephanie! What's the matter?"

Stephanie dropped her head down. "My cold. It's worse," she replied shakily. "I'm so . . . dizzy all of a sudden. Let me just stand here for— four minutes."

Joey put his arm around her. "Come on, let's go to the car. I'd better get you to a doctor."

"No!" she cried. "Er, I mean, what I really need is—" She glanced at her watch. One minute to eight. "Tea! I really need some tea!" She gazed at Joey, trying to appear as sick as possible. She threw in a few coughs.

"Tea?" Joey asked in confusion.

"Yes! Tea!" she replied, slightly annoyed.

"But, Stephanie, we're in a drugstore and you're coughing! Shouldn't I get you cough medicine?"

Good point, Stephanie thought. "Um, no, because . . . my heart is racing. I always cough when I'm nervous. I need to relax, and tea really helps me relax."

Joey stared at her as if she were crazy.

"Yes, a nice, hot cup of tea would make me much better." Stephanie turned her head toward the street. "Oh, and look: There's a coffee bar right next door! And they have tea too. And tea for two! And—"

"You really *do* need to relax," Joey told her. He put his arm around her and helped her into Perk Up.

"Thanks, Joey," she said. "I'll sit here and wait."

Joey hurried to the counter. Stephanie scanned the room.

Where was Natasha? She spotted a young woman a few tables away. The woman was sipping coffee and checking her watch. *Hmmm . . . She's pretty, and she seems to be waiting for some-*

body, Stephanie thought. But then a tall man sat down at her table.

Oops! Not her. Stephanie glanced around the room again. No one she saw was right. They were either too old, too young, or too plump to be a Russian ballerina.

Then she spotted her—a tall, leggy blonde. *Wow. She is really pretty! Joey is gonna love me for this!*

Stephanie hurried over and the blonde smiled at her. *Great smile*, Stephanie noted. "Hi!" she said to the woman. "I'm so happy to meet you!"

The blonde stared at Stephanie. "You are? Why? Whatta ya mean?"

Stephanie felt uneasy. She had expected the dancer to speak with a Russian accent.

"I said, I'm so happy to meet you. I'm Joey's friend. And he's excited to meet you too."

The woman eyed Stephanie strangely. "Who's Joey?"

"Uh, he's Lookin' for Love," Stephanie replied.

The woman stared. "Is this a joke?"

"No! I'm just trying to find Joey's date," Stephanie said. She noticed some people were watching them.

The woman picked up her coffee cup and

backed away nervously. "Well, I don't know who Joey is, or who you are, but I'm definitely *not* interested!" She leapt up and took a table as far from Stephanie as possible.

A commotion broke out in front of the store. Stephanie heard someone yelling, "Hey, lady! Cut it out!"

It was Joey's voice! Stephanie couldn't believe her eyes. A large woman in a black sweater was clobbering Joey over the head with her pocketbook.

"I am before you!" the woman shouted. "You not cut in front of me!"

Stephanie gulped. That woman had a foreign accent. Was it . . . Russian?

She raced over to Joey. He was trying to explain to the woman that he had been in line first.

"I did not cut in front of you," he repeated. "But I am in a hurry! I really need to get some tea for my sick friend."

"You are terrible man!" the woman cried. "You are not telling me truth!"

Everyone was staring. Stephanie couldn't believe it.

"You will not cut Natasha in line!" the woman

shouted. "I am big and strong. A dancer! See my muscles? I knock you to ground!"

Stephanie gasped. Natasha! She watched in shock as Natasha raised her pocketbook and threatened to club Joey over the head again. Stephanie jumped in quickly and pulled Joey away.

"Forget the tea," she cried. "I'm suddenly much better!"

"Good!" Joey replied. " 'Cause this lady is nuts!"

"Yes! Run from Natasha!" Natasha screamed after them. "Cowards!"

Back in the car, Stephanie stared out the window as Joey drove home. *What a close call that was!* She shuddered. It was hard to believe that Natasha was the woman she'd been dreaming about. What a terrible joke!

Thank goodness I didn't have to tell Joey that Natasha was his date for the evening! She could imagine how surprised Joey would have been. In fact, this whole dating business was turning into a big surprise. One bad surprise after the other. *Well, there's one good thing,* Stephanie told herself. *At least date number three can't possibly be worse than this!*

CHAPTER
12

♦ ◀ ✦ ♦

The next day Stephanie's father picked her up after her new jazz dance class. He wanted to give her a ride home before heading back to work. Stephanie knew he had another long night ahead of him, preparing for a special show at the TV station.

Stephanie had told him all about her earth science project. Danny was telling her everything he knew about the rain forest. Stephanie barely heard him. She was too nervous about Joey's next date. Dr. Lee Gatsby—Ms. Perfect!

Danny was still speaking as Stephanie jumped out of the car. "And don't forget to research the iguana—" was the last thing she heard. She raced into the house. She had to move fast. Her dad had stopped for gas on the way and now she was running really late.

Inside, Michelle was sprawled on the couch. A glass of milk and some cookies were placed neatly on a tray on the coffee table in front of her.

"Joey's home, right?" Stephanie asked as she rushed for the stairs.

"Yes. He's in the kitchen with D.J.," Michelle answered. "But Uncle Jesse and Aunt Becky took the twins to the—"

"Fine, fine," Stephanie muttered. She didn't need to hear anything more. She flew into her bedroom, flung her dance bag on the bed, and checked the time.

"A quarter to five!" she cried. "Oh, why did I make Joey's date for five o'clock?" She stared down at the big shirt she had thrown over her leggings and leotard. There was no time to change into something nicer. Anyway, what mattered was how *Joey* looked.

Now for her plan. Stephanie flung open her closet doors. She reached to the closet's top shelf and took down an armload of old textbooks. She scattered them over the floor. Next she pulled down a box of old shoes and sneakers and threw them around too.

Michelle walked in. "Stephanie? What are you doing?"

Stephanie pulled some clothing off their hangers and dropped them into a heap at her feet.

"Are you moving out of our room?" Michelle asked.

"No such luck," Stephanie replied.

"Then why are you throwing your things all over the place?"

Stephanie pushed her bangs off her face and took a deep breath. "Michelle, I don't have time to explain right now. Just sit on your bed and be quiet."

"Boy, are you moody!" Michelle sat on her bed while Stephanie pulled her desk chair over to the closet. She piled some heavy textbooks onto the chair.

"There. That should do it," Stephanie said. "Okay, I'm ready. Don't say anything!" she warned Michelle.

Stephanie picked up the back legs of her desk chair. The pile of books crashed to the floor, making an enormous noise.

Michelle stared wide-eyed at her sister. "Are you crazy?"

Stephanie let out a long, loud wail.

"Yup. You're crazy," Michelle said.

Stephanie cried louder and louder. Joey and D.J. rushed into the room. Stephanie sat on the floor of her closet, holding her arm and writhing in pain.

"Stephanie, what happened?" Joey asked in alarm.

"My wrist!" Stephanie cried. "Ooow! I think it's broken! Ooow!"

Joey knelt beside her. "Can you bend it?"

Stephanie pretended to try. "No! Oh, the pain! The pain! Quick, take me to the emergency room at San Francisco General Hospital!"

"Steph, honey, don't worry! I'll get you there right away. Just hang on, sweetie!" Joey helped her to her feet.

"Joey, the Wilson Clinic is only a minute away," D.J. told him. "Better go there."

"Noooo!" Stephanie screeched. "Not the Wilson Clinic! San Francisco General! It's—it's much better!"

D.J. shrugged. She and Michelle followed Joey and Stephanie to the top of the stairs. Stephanie glanced back and saw Michelle's stunned expression. She held a finger to her lips when Joey wasn't looking. "Don't worry," she mouthed to her sisters.

"Hang on, Steph, you're doing fine," Joey told her as they climbed down the steps. "I'll have you at the Wilson Clinic in a jiffy."

Stephanie had to think fast. She hadn't realized that another hospital might be closer to her house than San Francisco General.

"But I really want San Francisco General!" she insisted. "It's the only place I trust. Allie went there when she broke her arm last year. And Darcy went there when she had that stomach thing. And my friend from dance class once twisted her ankle and—"

Joey helped her into the front seat of his car. He hurried around to the driver's seat. "Okay, okay!" he said finally. "If it makes you happy, we'll go to San Francisco General. You'll feel better in no time."

Stephanie sniffled. "Thanks, Joey. Now I'm sure I will."

Stephanie paced impatiently across the waiting room at San Francisco General Hospital.

"This is ridiculous!" she cried. She held up her wrist and waved it at Joey. "I have a possible broken wrist here. How much longer do we have to wait?"

"Steph, calm down," Joey pleaded. "The nurses gave you an ice pack. Just keep it on your wrist until the doctor can see you. This complaining is crazy."

Stephanie sighed and grabbed the ice pack. "A person could go crazy waiting here," she grumbled.

"How long have we been waiting anyway?" Joey asked.

Stephanie turned her wrist to glance at her watch. She completely forgot that she was supposed to be in pain. "Almost a half hour!" she cried in disbelief. She noticed Joey staring at her arm.

"Oh, my wrist! Oooh, that hurt!" She paced over to the nurse's desk. "Excuse me," she said in a low voice. "I asked to see Dr. Gatsby a half hour ago."

"Dr. Gatsby is on a dinner break, miss," the nurse explained. "Dr. Kirschner is seeing emergencies now."

Stephanie groaned. She knew that Dr. Gatsby was on a dinner break. That's why she'd arranged the date for five o'clock. So Joey and Dr. Gatsby could meet over dinner.

"Please, Dr. Gatsby told me to use the hospital page when I got here," Stephanie insisted.

"Dr. Gatsby knew you were going to injure your wrist?" The nurse stared at Stephanie.

"Uh—no. But, uh, we're old friends. 'If you're ever in trouble, just page good old Dr. Gatsby, your pal.' That's our arrangement," Stephanie told the nurse. "And now I really need you to page Dr. Gatsby."

"I'm sorry, miss, but—"

Joey walked up to the desk. "Is there a problem?" he asked. "We've been waiting a long time. When can the doctor see her?"

The nurse checked her computer screen. "I already told her, Dr. Kirschner is available. You can see her now."

"No!" Stephanie said in a panic. "Dr. Gatsby is the best! I want Dr. Gatsby!"

"But, Stephanie—" Joey began.

The nurse's phone rang. She spoke into it briefly. "You're in luck, Miss Tanner," the nurse said as she hung up. "It seems Dr. Gatsby came back from dinner early. Why don't you go wait now in room three?"

Stephanie breathed a sigh of relief. "Well, it's about time!"

Joey helped Stephanie into room three and onto the examination table. The door opened and the doctor came in.

"Hello, I'm Dr. Gatsby," the doctor said. "My dinner date seems to have canceled, so I'm all yours. Now, what's the problem?"

Stephanie's mouth dropped open. She stared at the doctor. "But ... but ..."

Dr. Gatsby lifted Stephanie's wrist gently. "Where does it hurt?"

"You can't be Dr. Gatsby," Stephanie managed to say.

"I can't?"

Joey laughed. "Hey, a funny doctor!"

"But ... you're a man!" Stephanie blurted out.

Dr. Gatsby shrugged. "It's never been a problem before."

Joey laughed again.

Stephanie was dumbfounded. She turned to Joey. "Um, do you think that you could wait for me outside?" she asked.

Joey seemed surprised. "Are you sure, Steph?" he asked. "I don't mind waiting."

"Please," Stephanie begged.

"Well, sure, I guess. If that's what you want." Joey opened the door. "I'll be right out here if you need me."

When he was gone, Stephanie hopped off the table.

"Really, there's nothing to worry about," Dr. Gatsby said. "I won't hurt you. I promise."

"But how could you be a man?" Stephanie asked. "What about the personal ad?" She tapped her foot impatiently. "How come you answered it?"

Dr. Gatsby seemed shocked. "How do you know about that?" he asked.

"Because I wrote it! I set up this date—for Joey!" Stephanie leaned back against the table.

Dr. Gatsby was silent for a moment. Then he reached into his pocket and pulled out the magazine page. He pointed toward the waiting room. "You don't mean he's—"

"Lookin' for Love! I wrote the ad for Joey," she explained. "I was hoping to find him a date for Valentine's Day."

Dr. Gatsby read the ad again and chuckled. "Well, it's an honest mistake," he pointed out. "It doesn't say here that Lookin' for Love is a man. I thought he . . . I mean, she was a woman!"

"Can I see too?" Stephanie asked.

Dr. Gatsby handed her the ad. She read it over and groaned. Dr. Gatsby was right. The ad didn't say anything about Joey being a guy.

"I can't believe this," she mumbled.

"Uh, so I take it the broken wrist was just an act?" Dr. Gatsby asked.

Stephanie felt her face turn red. "Yeah. But if Joey finds out I was faking, he might be mad enough to break it for real!"

Dr. Gatsby grinned. He tapped the table with his hand. "Hop up," he instructed her. "Let me take another look at that wrist. Maybe I can find something wrong with it!"

Stephanie smiled as she leapt onto the table.

"Oh, yes," Dr. Gatsby muttered as he examined her arm. "I think I've pinpointed a possible relaxation of the radial nerve that causes a numbness of your extremity."

Stephanie's eyes widened. "That sounds serious."

Dr. Gatsby chuckled. "Don't worry," he whispered, "it just means your arm is asleep."

Stephanie giggled as he wrapped her wrist in an Ace bandage. At least she'd been right about one thing—Dr. Gatsby was pretty funny.

CHAPTER
13

◆ ◢ ◣ ◆

Up in her bedroom, Stephanie read the letter from dream date number four again—and again, just to be sure. No doubt about it—Risa was definitely a woman!

That's one thing that won't go wrong this time, Stephanie thought. She hid the letter at the back of her drawer. Yesterday's mix-up at the hospital had taught her one lesson—never assume anything. She'd assumed Dr. Gatsby was a woman, and she'd been wrong. Stephanie sighed deeply.

She'd been so sure about all the dates—and not one had worked out so far. She thought about the night before at the coffee bar. Who would have thought that a Russian dancer named Natasha could be such a major disappointment? And who could have dreamed that the fix-up with a chemistry teacher could go so wrong? She'd never even made it past the front door!

Fixing someone up was a lot harder than Stephanie had thought. So far Operation FUJG was one big, giant, total flop. If only tonight's date could go smoothly. Valentine's Day was only one day away! Date number four—Risa— was her very last hope!

Stephanie made a wish. *Please, please let Risa be the one! For Joey's sake!*

Stephanie could tell that Joey was feeling worse and worse the closer it was to Valentine's Day. Sure, he was putting up a good front, telling everyone he enjoyed hanging out with his guy friends. But he wasn't *acting* very happy.

Stephanie knew it had been especially hard for Joey this past week. Everybody in the house was making big plans for Valentine's Day. Her father had called Marvelous Marissa about a zillion times to plan their big night. Uncle Jesse kept bragging about buying great tickets to *Grease* for Aunt Becky. And D.J. actually had two dates. An afternoon coffee date with Ben the twin, and an evening date with some guy she'd met in the library. Stephanie wondered how her older sister was going to pull *that* off.

Stephanie felt bad for Joey, but she also felt pretty sorry for herself. It wasn't as though she had the world's greatest date lined up. Or *any* date, for that matter.

Kyle hadn't even spoken to her in school, except about earth science. Stephanie had told him everything she'd learned so far about the rain forest—including the dating habits of the iguana. Kyle hadn't gotten the hint. They *had* made a sort of date—to talk more about the project. But that wouldn't happen until the following week.

It made Stephanie very nervous. Because, like it or not, in only twenty-four hours Kyle would hear her Valentine's Day message on the radio!

It had taken all her nerve to give Joey the written valentine to take to the station. Her heart had been thumping a mile a minute. But she had written it and she had signed it. After all, as Allie had said, what was the point of sending it if Kyle didn't know who it was from?

Now she could only wait to see what happened. One way or another, Valentine's Day would be a big day for her. A possible monumental event in her future relationship with Kyle Sullivan!

The phone rang and seconds later D.J. yelled up to her.

"Steph! Phone!"

Stephanie hurried into her father's room to answer. "Hello?"

"Stephanie! You have to come save me! I'm losing my mind!"

"Allie!" Stephanie laughed. "Things can't be that bad."

"They are!" Allie insisted. "I thought things were bad when Aunt Wendy was sulking in her bathrobe and crying all day. But this is worse. Check it out—Aunt Wendy is hooked on infomercials!"

"Huh?" Stephanie asked.

"Infomercials," Allie repeated. "Those really long commercials that are on TV late at night. You know, where they try to sell you things that will change your life? This week alone Aunt Wendy has bought a complete set of Miracle Makeover Makeup, a deluxe Peel Your Way to Beauty facial kit, and a Complete Body Toner exercise machine!"

"Oh," Stephanie said.

"More like 'Oh no!'" Allie groaned. "This afternoon the postman delivered some strange-looking contraption. Turns out it's called the Hair We Go. Aunt Wendy ordered it—and now she wants to try it out. On *me!*"

"You're kidding!"

"She's heating it up right now! I don't think I can go through with it, Steph," Allie cried. "I mean, I didn't mind the makeup makeover, or the peach-flavored facial. Or even the exercise routine. But I like my hair the way it is!"

"Well, dream date number four is coming here at eight-thirty," Stephanie said. "I have to stay to make sure that it isn't another disaster. I mean, it would be nice if Joey actually met this woman."

"I understand," Allie said, trying not to sound disappointed.

"But the way these dates are going, it'll probably be over in about three minutes," Stephanie continued. "So I could drop by afterward and keep you company. Okay?"

"That would be awesome! You promise?" Allie asked.

"Promise," Stephanie replied.

Allie sighed with relief. "I feel tons better. Thanks. How's Joey holding up, by the way?"

"He doesn't suspect a thing," Stephanie said.

"Of course not." Allie giggled. "He has no idea he's been fixed up three times already this week!"

Stephanie tried to laugh, but failed. She couldn't help feeling gloomy about date number four. "Well, it would be nice if this one worked out," Stephanie said.

"Isn't this the date who used to be a comedy writer?" Allie asked. "That means she's got a sense of humor."

"Yeah. That means if this date's a bust, at least she might laugh about it." Stephanie sighed. She was beginning to sigh as much as Joey.

"Think positively," Allie advised. "This could be the one date that works out. Joey and number four might even fall in love. And all because of you! He'll be so grateful, he might buy you a new stereo! Or a new car! Or maybe he'll send you on a world cruise!"

"Allie, aren't you jumping the gun a bit?" Stephanie asked. "I mean, they haven't even met and you already have me packing!"

"I know," Allie said. "But it *could* work out."

"I've said that three times already. Anyway, I'd better hang up," Stephanie said. "I have more important things to worry about. Like, how am I going to get everybody out of the house tonight so Joey and his dream date can have a minute alone?"

"Don't forget to come over later," Allie reminded her. "We have a date—to destroy the Hair We Go!"

It was a quiet Friday evening at the Tanner house. Much quieter than it had been in a long time, Stephanie realized. She glanced at her watch. Ten after eight! And everyone was still home. Usually, on Fridays, everyone was running around, getting ready to go out. Tonight everyone was sitting around as if they had nowhere to go.

Stephanie found her aunt Becky and uncle Jesse in the kitchen, trying to coax the twins into finishing dinner.

"Come on, Alex," Jesse pleaded. "You love broccoli, remember?"

"Come on, Nicky," Becky pleaded. "You love sweet potatoes, remember?"

Nicky and Alex covered their mouths with

their hands. Jesse and Becky exchanged frustrated glances.

"Wait! I've got it!" Jesse announced. He switched both dinner plates. Seconds later Nicky was grabbing for broccoli while Alex was happily eating up the sweet potatoes.

"Jess, you're a genius!" Becky exclaimed.

Jesse ran his fingers through his hair. "Yeah, I know."

"Daddy, you just put sweet potatoes in your hair!" Nicky cried.

Jesse reached up to feel his hair. "Yech!" he said, running to the sink.

Stephanie ran to get him a towel. "So, Uncle Jesse, since you're washing your hair, why don't you and Aunt Becky go out tonight?" she asked. "I'll baby-sit. For free! Stay out as late as you want!"

Jesse pulled his wet head out of the sink. "Thanks, but no thanks, Steph. We're both beat tonight. We'll just stay in and watch a movie."

D.J. hurried into the kitchen.

"Deej! So, who's your date with tonight?" Stephanie raised her eyebrows a few times. "Ben, Glen, or Len?" she teased.

"Relax, Stephanie," D.J. answered. "I don't

have a date tonight." She took out a can of cola from the refrigerator. Then she pulled the popcorn maker from the pantry. "I have a major exam on Monday. I have to study all night tonight so I can go out tomorrow night."

"Go out twice," Stephanie reminded her.

"You have two dates?" Becky asked with a laugh. "How exactly are you going to manage that?"

D.J. flicked on the popcorn maker. "Ben is taking me out for an early coffee date. Then he has to go home and study. But Randy is coming over to pick me up later."

Stephanie felt a pang of jealousy. D.J. had two dates for Valentine's Day, while she didn't even have one. She glanced at her watch and gulped. She didn't have time to think about that. It was almost eight-thirty! Dream date number four would be there any minute. And where was Joey?

CHAPTER
14

◆ ◢ ◂ ◆

Stephanie flew into the living room. Things didn't look too promising. Danny and Joey were slumped on the sofa, watching television. Michelle was on the floor, flipping through the pages of a magazine that couldn't possibly interest her.

"Michelle, aren't you going to Josh's tonight?" Stephanie asked hopefully.

Michelle shook her head. "No. I hate Josh," she replied.

"I thought he was your best friend," Stephanie said.

"He's my *ex*-best friend," Michelle said.

"We're not talking anymore. Not since he started talking to Karen Hardy. I hate her because she's friends with Lisa Percy."

Stephanie rolled her eyes. "Well, what about Cassie? She's still your friend, right?"

Michelle nodded.

Stephanie sat down next to her and whispered. "Here's five bucks. Rent some movies and go to Cassie's tonight."

"I can't," Michelle said. "No one will drive me. They're all staying in tonight."

"You have legs, right? Walk over!"

"She lives too far to walk," Michelle protested.

"Then take your bike. Take my bike if you have to!"

"But . . . it's nighttime!"

Stephanie shoved the five dollars back into her pocket. "Never mind," she grumbled. At least her father would be going out.

"So, Dad," she said brightly. "Where are you and Marvel . . . uh, I mean Marissa, going tonight?"

"Nowhere. We're not going out tonight. Or any other night, ever again." Her father shook his head sadly.

She gazed at him in astonishment. "What happened?"

"It's over with Marvelous—I mean Marissa," he said. "She broke our big Valentine's night date. And with a very lame excuse," he added. "She called to say she had a bad cold and had lost her voice. But by the end of the conversation she was practically yelling in my ear." He slumped even lower on the couch. "I know when I've been dumped."

"Oh, Dad—that's terrible," Stephanie said.

Joey put his arm around Danny's shoulders. "Not to worry. Me and Dan the Man here are going to hang out together tonight and every night. Just two ol' college buddies goofin' around. We don't need dates. We'll enjoy our own kind of Valentine's Day. Valentine's for good friends."

Danny smiled and put his arm around Joey too. "Yeah. Who needs dates anyway?"

Stephanie groaned. *Not this again!* This was *not* what Joey needed to hear right now. Joey should be thinking how great it would be to meet the girl of his dreams!

"Uh, Dad, maybe it's not a good idea for you to hang around with Joey. I mean, maybe you need to get your mind off Marissa. What about a nice long car ride?" she suggested.

"But it's pouring rain," Danny pointed out.

"So? You'll be in the car. You won't get wet."

"No. The brakes have sounded funny lately. I don't want to take any chances on wet roads," Danny said.

"Well, maybe you can rent a car! Don't they have one-night rental rates?"

Danny stared at her. "Stephanie, what are you talking about?"

Stephanie knew she was talking crazy. But she was starting to panic. Uncle Jesse and Aunt Becky weren't going out. D.J. wasn't going out. Her father wasn't going out. Even Michelle wasn't going out! It was going to be an awfully full house for Joey's big chance to be alone with his possibly perfect match.

She'd really hoped Joey and Risa could spend five minutes alone. Instead, their magic meeting was going to take place in front of an audience!

The front doorbell rang. Stephanie glanced at her watch. Eight-thirty exactly. At least Risa was punctual.

"Joey!" she cried. "Uh, your turn to answer the door!"

Joey ignored her. Danny stood up to answer the door. "Are we expecting anyone?" he asked as he turned the knob. He flung the door open wide.

An absolutely gorgeous woman stood on the front step. Stephanie saw her father's eyes light up instantly.

"Marissa!" he cried. "You're here!"

Marissa? Stephanie stared.

Marissa stared at Stephanie's father. "D-Danny?" She had a bewildered look on her face. "Are you . . . Lookin' for Love?"

Danny smiled and winked. "I sure am, sweetie pie!"

Stephanie's mouth dropped open in shock. *Marvelous Marissa . . . Risa . . . oh, no!*

"I'm so glad you changed your mind," Danny said happily. He reached out to give her a hug. "Everyone, this is Marvel—uh, Marissa Brooks!"

Michelle and D.J. hurried in from the kitchen, followed by Becky, Jesse, and the twins. They all waved a greeting and gawked at Marvelous Marissa.

"But . . . the ad . . . how did you . . ." Marissa seemed confused.

"Come to think of it, Marissa," Danny said suddenly, "how did you find my house? I didn't think you knew my address."

"I . . . I . . ." Marissa seemed stunned. "I'm not sure I understand," she finally said. "Why did you write that ad anyway?"

"Ad?" Danny stared at her. "What ad?"

Stephanie swallowed loudly, then cleared her throat. "I . . . I think I can explain," she said meekly. She glanced awkwardly at Marissa. "I put the ad in the magazine," she told her. "But not for my dad. For Joey."

"Huh?" Joey glanced up from the couch. "For me?"

"For him?" Marissa stared at Joey and then back at Danny in confusion. "But who's he?"

"What ad?" Danny demanded. "What magazine? What is going on?"

Stephanie's cheeks burned. She stared down at the floor. Her entire family stood there, gaping at her.

"I took out a personal ad in *San Francisco Scene* magazine," Stephanie explained. "To find Joey a date."

Joey's jaw dropped open. "I don't believe it!"

"I signed it 'Lookin' for Love'," Stephanie

went on. "I set up some dates for Joey, and, well, Risa—I mean Marissa—turned out to be one of them." Stephanie gave her father a pleading look. "Dad, I really didn't know she was your Marissa. She said her name was Risa!"

Danny shot a look at Marissa. "Is this true?"

"Well, uh, I—" Marissa sputtered in embarrassment. "My nickname used to be Risa," she finally said.

Danny seemed heartbroken all over again. He could barely look at Marissa. His voice dropped to a whisper. "You answered a personal ad while we were dating?"

"Well, we went on only two dates," Marissa said. "It isn't like we were seeing each other a long time. And anyway, I . . . you . . . I . . ." Marissa hung her head. "I think I should go now. I'm sorry, Danny. Really. For everything."

The door closed behind her. A second later they heard Marissa's car speeding away from the house.

Danny forced a smile. "Well. How do you like that?"

Stephanie felt awful. "I'm sorry, Dad. Really sorry."

"Uh, Stephanie?" Joey asked.

Stephanie gulped. She'd been so concerned for her father's feelings, she'd almost forgotten about Joey. His voice sounded really strange. He didn't look too happy either.

"Would you mind explaining that part about the personal ad—one more time?" he asked.

Stephanie laughed nervously. "Oh, right. The personal ad!" She shifted from one foot to the other. Joey glared at her, waiting for an explanation.

She took a deep breath. "It's all because of Valentine's Day," she blurted out. "I mean, I knew how badly I felt, not having a valentine. And I knew you were lonely too, Joey. I mean, at least I had the radio show. I could send a valentine to the guy I like. But what could you do?"

Joey looked less and less happy.

"I was feeling so bad for you," Stephanie continued. "Watching you sulk around the house and sighing all the time. I wanted to help. So I wrote the personal ad to find you a date."

Danny shook his head at her sadly. "I know you meant well, Stephanie. But you should learn not to meddle. You did harm instead of good."

Stephanie felt awful. Joey was still without a

valentine. And now her father was without one too. "Are you very upset about Marissa, Dad?"

"I wish things had worked out differently," Danny admitted. "But I guess this proved that Marissa wasn't so marvelous after all. Not to me anyway. Maybe you did me a favor."

Stephanie felt a wave of relief. "I'll still be your valentine," she told her dad. "And so will Joey. And D.J. and Michelle and—"

"I know, I know." Danny grinned. "Don't worry about me. And don't put any ads in the magazine for me either. How many women answered, by the way?"

"About a thousand," Stephanie told him.

Danny seemed stunned. "A thousand?" he cried.

"A thousand?" Joey echoed.

"Well, it was a pretty good ad," Stephanie boasted. "I made Joey sound like an awesome catch."

Joey narrowed his eyes.

"I mean, you *are* an awesome catch," Stephanie quickly told him. "I didn't have to lie or anything. And, boy, it was hard work reading all of those letters. But we narrowed it down to just a few for your blind dates. Too bad none of them worked out so well."

Joey seemed confused. "What blind dates?"

Uh-oh. Stephanie took a deep breath before explaining everything to Joey. About how he'd already met a chemistry teacher, a Russian dancer, and a doctor before meeting Marissa. And without even knowing it!

"I'm really sorry, Joey," she finished. "I mean, I was hoping this would all turn out . . . well . . . better."

Joey's expression was suddenly angrier than before.

Stephanie felt as if she might cry. "Joey, I was only trying to help!"

"Don't you realize how embarrassed I am? How could you do that to me?" Joey walked toward the stairs. "Do me a favor, Stephanie," he called over his shoulder. "Don't do me any more favors."

CHAPTER
15

◆ ◂ ✦ ◆

It was Valentine's Day. Stephanie had circled the date on her calendar and colored over it with a big red heart. "Big day!!" she had scrawled across it. Now she took a black marker and crossed the date off. *Big deal*, she thought. She had spent the whole day in her room, feeling sorry for herself. She'd gone downstairs a few times, but Joey's silent treatment was enough to make her run back up.

Just before dinner Michelle tiptoed into the bedroom. She leaned over Stephanie, who was lying facedown on her bed.

"Joey is still really mad at you," Michelle said.

Stephanie rolled onto her back and stared at the ceiling. "Thanks for the update, Michelle. But I think I already knew that."

Michelle flopped down on her own bed. "What are you going to do now?"

Stephanie sighed. "What *can* I do?" She didn't know how to make things better. She'd really blown it this time. Joey was still feeling horrible, and she was feeling even worse.

She clutched her pillow tightly. How had such a good idea turned into such a mess?

There was a knock on the door. Stephanie sat up quickly. "Joey?" she called hopefully.

The door opened and Allie rushed in. When Stephanie saw her, she laughed out loud despite her awful mood. Half of Allie's head was covered with thick, bouncy curls. The other half was as straight as a stick. She looked like one of those "Don't do this" photos in a fashion magazine.

Michelle stared. "What happened to you?" she asked.

"Not Aunt Wendy and the Hair You Go?" Stephanie asked.

Allie nodded miserably. She held up a big pink baseball cap. "I had to hide under this hat all day!"

Stephanie winced. "I'm really sorry I couldn't make it last night," she said. "Maybe I could've stopped her."

"Forget it. No one could stop Aunt Wendy." Allie sank onto the bed next to Stephanie. "I'm just sorry things went so wrong with Joey."

Stephanie had called Allie late the previous night to explain why she couldn't drop by. It was still hard to believe they had fixed up Joey with her dad's new girlfriend. But how could they have known that Marvelous Marissa was really Risa, the comedy writer? Or that Marissa would break a date with Danny so that she could meet Lookin' for Love? Or that . . . Stephanie shuddered. It was all too terrible to think about.

"How'd you get away from your aunt anyway?" Stephanie asked Allie.

"She ordered this Health Spa in a Can bubble bath," Allie explained. "I finally convinced her to try it out. As soon as she started soaking, I made a run for it!"

"Well, I might make a run for it too," Stephanie told her. "My dad's not too upset about Marissa, but Joey's still not speaking to me. And now *neither* of them have valentines, and it's all my fault." She rested her chin in her hands.

Downstairs, the doorbell rang. "Who could that be?" Stephanie murmured.

"At least it's not another dream date," Michelle said.

Stephanie fell back on her pillow, then bolted up in a panic. "Oh, no!" she cried.

"What's wrong?" Allie asked in alarm.

Stephanie grabbed Allie's arms. She stared at her in complete horror. "I totally forgot!"

"Forgot what?" Allie asked.

Stephanie felt sick to her stomach. "It *is* another dream date! Dream date number five!"

Allie gasped. "What?"

"Remember, I made the last date for tonight. So Joey would have a date for Valentine's Day— in case Risa didn't work out. I can't believe I forgot to call and cancel!" She groaned in dismay.

"Which one is it?" Allie asked.

"Short and Snappy! The woman who wrote 'I'm the one. Call me.' The one Darcy thought was so funny. The one who signed herself 'Lookin' for Love Too.' Oh, Allie, help me! What am I going to do?" Stephanie groaned loudly. "And what's Joey going to do to me?"

Allie grabbed Stephanie by the arm and pulled

her to the stairs. "We'll think of something," she cried. "Let's get down there fast! Before any more damage is done!"

Stephanie and Allie raced downstairs. About halfway down, they both stopped short. Joey was already at the front door.

Stephanie couldn't believe her eyes! He was hugging a gorgeous woman in a little black dress!

"Aunt Wendy!" Allie cried.

"Aunt Wendy?" Stephanie's eyes widened. *That's* Aunt Wendy?" She gaped in amazement. It couldn't be! Could this terrific-looking person hugging Joey be the same soggy slob who'd been moping around Allie's house last weekend?

Joey glanced up and noticed Stephanie and Allie on the staircase. He beamed at them.

At least Joey seems to have forgotten he was furious with me, Stephanie thought.

"Look, you guys!" Joey called excitedly. "It's Wendy Madison! She went to college with me and your dad!" Joey blushed like a little kid. "I had a crush on her for the longest time!"

Stephanie felt her mouth drop open. "Really?" she managed to say.

"Allie?" Wendy stared at her niece in surprise. "What are you doing here?"

"Me?" Allie asked in shock. "What are *you* doing here? And all dressed up!"

"Wait a minute," Joey said. "How do you two know each other?"

Stephanie stepped forward. "Joey, I think I can explain—"

Joey groaned loudly. "Oh, no. Don't tell me you had something to do with this!"

"No! I didn't do anything! Aunt Wendy probably came here to make Allie go home. Really," Stephanie cried.

Joey stared at Wendy. "You're Allie's aunt?"

Wendy nodded.

"Wow! What a coincidence!" Joey grinned even wider than before. "That's wild. And you came to pick up Allie?"

"Well, no," Wendy said, looking uncomfortable. "Actually, I'm kind of here in response to . . . a personal ad."

Stephanie and Allie exchanged stunned glances.

Joey seemed stunned too. "Don't tell me," he gulped. "Are you here to meet Lookin' for Love?"

Wendy's face turned red. "I am," she confessed.

"So am I!" Joey cried. "I mean, that's me! I

mean, actually, it was Stephanie, but it was *supposed* to be me—"

Joey stopped in confusion. Wendy stared at him in disbelief, then turned to stare at Stephanie.

Stephanie stared back at Wendy, then at Allie, then at Joey. They all burst out laughing.

"This is too weird!" Allie cried. "Aunt Wendy, why did you answer that ad?"

Wendy blushed. "I finally realized I'd spent enough time sulking. You can't hang out in pajamas feeling sorry for yourself forever. Sometimes you have to pick yourself up and do something positive."

Stephanie and Joey exchanged knowing glances. "I agree with that," Joey murmured.

"I can't believe we picked my aunt Wendy out of a thousand letters!" Allie exclaimed.

"Well, I'm awfully glad you did." Joey smiled broadly at Wendy. "It sure is great to see you again! And looking so terrific."

"Thanks to Miracle Makeup, Peel Your Way to Beauty, and Health Spa in a Can," Wendy joked.

Stephanie and Allie grinned at each other. "We did it," Stephanie whispered. "We made the perfect match! And just in time for Valentine's Day!" Stephanie turned to Joey.

"I'm really truly sorry for what I did, Joey," she said. "I never meant to embarrass you. I only wanted to help."

Joey reached out and gave her a big hug. "I know, Steph. I was feeling kind of sorry for myself lately. That's why I got so mad at you. I see now that you were trying to cheer me up."

Stephanie sighed with relief. "So, Happy Valentine's Day?"

"Happy Valentine's Day, Steph," Joey replied. "And speaking of valentines, shouldn't you be listening to the radio? Your Valentine's Day message—"

"Yikes!" Stephanie slapped her forehead. She grabbed Allie and dragged her over to the stereo. She flicked it on and turned the volume up high.

"What if they played it already?" she cried. "What if we missed the whole thing?"

Three messages later, the deejay announced: "And now, for all you listeners from John Muir Middle School."

Stephanie screamed. "This is it!"

"I'm so excited!" Allie exclaimed. "I still can't believe you really sent it!"

"Neither can I!" Stephanie squealed.

The deejay began to read: "A special valentine message for Kyle Sullivan. Red are the roses, green is the grass. You have an admirer in your earth science class."

Stephanie and Allie jumped up and down, shrieking.

"You did it!" Allie cried. "You really did it!"

The phone rang and Joey answered it. "Valentines Central," he joked. "Steph . . . it's for you. It's—"

Joey didn't have to finish. Stephanie could hear Darcy's screams as clearly as if she were standing three feet away.

"Stephanie!" Darcy cried when Stephanie took the phone. "Wasn't it wild to hear that on the air?"

"The wildest!" Stephanie agreed.

Allie threw an arm around Stephanie. That was a gutsy thing to do. And maybe now—"

"Shhhh!" Stephanie interrupted. *Did I just hear what I thought I heard?*

"Was that your name on the radio—again?" Darcy squawked over the phone.

Stephanie and Allie crowded closer to the stereo.

". . . and I couldn't have picked a better—or cuter—earth science partner! Happy Valentine's Day!" The deejay paused. "Once again, that sweet message goes out to Stephanie Tanner from Kyle Sullivan. Looks like we have one perfect match here, folks! Happy Valentine's Day to everyone!"

For a moment there was total silence as Stephanie stared at Allie in shock. Darcy's voice squealed through the telephone that Stephanie clutched in her hand.

"Wow," Stephanie finally said. "At last—a fix-up that *wasn't* a mix-up!"

Then she, Allie, and Darcy started screaming all over again.

FULL HOUSE Stephanie™

PHONE CALL FROM A FLAMINGO	88004-7/$3.99
THE BOY-OH-BOY NEXT DOOR	88121-3/$3.99
TWIN TROUBLES	88290-2/$3.99
HIP HOP TILL YOU DROP	88291-0/$3.99
HERE COMES THE BRAND NEW ME	89858-2/$3.99
THE SECRET'S OUT	89859-0/$3.99
DADDY'S NOT-SO-LITTLE GIRL	89860-4/$3.99
P.S. FRIENDS FOREVER	89861-2/$3.99
GETTING EVEN WITH THE FLAMINGOES	52273-6/$3.99
THE DUDE OF MY DREAMS	52274-4/$3.99
BACK-TO-SCHOOL COOL	52275-2/$3.99
PICTURE ME FAMOUS	52276-0/$3.99
TWO-FOR-ONE CHRISTMAS FUN	53546-3/$3.99
THE BIG FIX-UP MIX-UP	53547-1/$3.99
TEN WAYS TO WRECK A DATE	53548-X/$3.99
WISH UPON A VCR	53549-8/$3.99
DOUBLES OR NOTHING	56841-8/$3.99
SUGAR AND SPICE ADVICE	56842-6/$3.99
NEVER TRUST A FLAMINGO	56843-4/$3.99
THE TRUTH ABOUT BOYS	00361-5/$3.99
CRAZY ABOUT THE FUTURE	00362-3/$3.99
MY SECRET ADMIRER	00363-1/$3.99
BLUE RIBBON CHRISTMAS	00830-7/$3.99
THE STORY ON OLDER BOYS	00831-5/$3.99
MY THREE WEEKS AS A SPY	00832-3/$3.99

Available from Minstrel® Books Published by Pocket Books